UNDERGROUND

BY BETH BROWN

IRON CAULDRON BOOKS
www.IronCauldronBooks.com

Any of the titles from Iron Cauldron Books may be purchased for education, business, or sales promotional use. For information, please write:

Special Markets Department, Iron Cauldron Books, 2209 Fenton Street, Richmond, VA 23231.

First edition.

Library of Congress Cataloging-in-Publication Data
Brown, Beth.
  Underground / by Beth Brown
    p. cm.

    ISBN-13: 978-0-9895560-0-2 (paperback)
    ISBN-10: 0-9895560-0-X (paperback)
    I. Title.

11 12 13 14 15 ICB 10 9 8 7 6 5 4 3 2 1

ACKNOWLEDGEMENTS

The list of people deserving of thanks for their patience, kindness, sympathy, help, and friendship during the creation of this book is a long one. Though not everyone is mentioned individually, you can bet that not a single one of you was forgotten.

First, I owe a debt of gratitude to Chris Baty and his team of dedicated lunatics who started— and perpetuate—National Novel Writing Month (NaNoWriMo.) Every year, droves of writers, both amateur and professional, race to complete a fifty-thousand word novel in only thirty days. *Underground* began as a NaNoWriMo project, but I quickly felt something in the story that I wanted to nurture and tend for more than one short month. Five years later, because of the crazy "month of literary abandon" that Baty and friends unleashed on the world, I have a book that I'm proud of.

Many thanks go to all of my friends and fans who showed that they cared enough about the creation of this book to make a pledge in my name to the Office of Letters and Light, the non-profit entity that manages and executes NaNoWriMo. Your kind contributions are helping to make thousands of young writers as happy as you've made me.

I'm grateful for all of the wonderful authors I have worked with these last few years who encouraged and inspired me (whether you knew it or not) to get through the tough times and tell the story I was compelled to tell. Dale Brumfield, Theresa Clinton, Phil Ford, Patrick Ohlde, Katie Mullaly—you're all too cool for your own good.

I would be nuts not to thank Brian Byers for all of his creative empowerment over the course of this and many other projects. He's a man with a million-and-one ideas, but he puts his love of seeing other people make awesome things as his top priority. I hope I can someday be the creative force that Brian thinks I am.

I am forever beholden to Ruth Perkinson and her inspirational group of Featherstone Writers. You all gave me the push to the finish line that I so desperately needed, but you did it with such gusto that I hardly knew what hit me. Best wishes to all of you with your own works in progress, and I hope that I can someday impact other writers' lives the way you all have impacted mine.

Finally, I extend immeasurable love and appreciation to my husband and kids. You were right beside me from start to finish—even through those difficult test reads, the months of my pacing the floor while pondering plot, and the late dinners. I couldn't have done any of this without your support.

CHAPTER 1

"It's wild, isn't it? Only three blocks away!" Emily's mom chattered into the telephone. "I know. It could have been anywhere on this stretch of the hill. Swallowed up two cars! How did the city not see a disaster like this coming?"

Emily absorbed her mother's side of the conversation while gulping down breakfast and studying the aerial images on the morning news. Sometime just before dawn, the street had collapsed right around the corner and left a gaping hole large enough to swallow her house. The news anchor talked about all kinds of reasons the sinkhole could have occurred where it did—old train tunnels under Church Hill losing their stability, too much rain recently creating pockets of water underground, even something about secret Confederate bunkers and munitions storage that could have been lost and forgotten. Emily didn't really care; this was the most exciting thing to happen in her neighborhood the entire time she lived there.

She cleaned up her breakfast dishes and gave her mom a wave before darting out the back door. She ran four houses down through the alley and ducked through an old wooden gate. Sarah met her at the back door.

"Did you hear what our moms were talking about?" Sarah asked with wide eyes.

"Yeah, let's go see it!" Emily answered.

"Hang on, I want to go get my camera. She said that two cars got sucked down into the road when it cracked. That *has* to go in the scrapbook." Sarah disappeared back into the house for only a moment and returned to burst out of the old screen door.

The two girls ran out of the alley to the old brick sidewalk on 28th Street. It was pretty obvious by watching which direction everyone was walking their dogs this morning where to find the latest arrival to the neighborhood. They followed the slow trickle of people east, speculating the entire time about what they might find when they got to their destination.

Emily and Sarah had been best friends for four years, which was a pretty long time when you're only eleven and thirteen years old. Sarah's family had inherited their house on Franklin Street from her great-grandparents and had lived there since long before she was born. Emily and her parents moved to Grace Street when she was only three.

Both girls were homeschooled and kept mainly to themselves during the day. They didn't even realize they had so much in common with someone so close until their mothers ran into each other at a local meeting for homeschooling parents. The rest, as far as Emily and Sarah were concerned, was destiny.

The crowd near the sinkhole was thick. City public utility workers and Richmond Police and Fire had already been there for several hours and had roped off the area with ugly yellow plastic tape to keep spectators at a safe distance. Unfortunately, that "safe" distance also meant you couldn't see a thing. The girls snaked through the onlookers and made their way to the tape at the front, but no matter how much they craned their necks in an attempt to get a better look, all they could see were fire trucks sitting near lots of asphalt triangles pointing in unnatural directions. Sarah twisted her curly brown hair for a moment and then said, "I have an idea! Let's go to Vivian's house and see if we can go up on her balcony."

It was much more work to get *out* of the crowd than it was to get in. They exchanged dozens of excuse me's before finally making their way back to the sidewalk. Vivian lived only four houses down, but it took almost five minutes to walk there through all of the chatting neighbors. She spotted

Emily and Sarah as they approached and waved them up to her porch with much enthusiasm.

"Isn't it *cool*?" Vivian squealed. "Our whole house shook last night! My dad thought someone blew up a car and came running outside just in time to see Mr. Hinson's truck going under the road. I guess we're lucky it happened down at the traffic circle instead of on the narrow part of the street here—one of the houses could have fallen in instead of just cars!" She was so enthusiastic about the whole disaster that she made it seem like some kind of celebrity had moved in next door. Emily and Sarah exchanged what-the-heck glances as Emily worked up the nerve to ask Vivian about the third floor balcony.

"We tried to get close, but couldn't see a thing because of the fire trucks. Do you think we could all go up to your top balcony and try and get some pictures for the neighborhood scrapbook?" she asked.

Vivian suddenly had a look of surprise like she had just won a bingo jackpot. "I completely forgot about that! It's a great idea, come on." The three ducked past Vivian's parents and some neighbors talking and laughing near the front door and headed for the stairs. This house was much older and grander than Emily or Sarah's, and as a result had a lot more steps. Breathless and with hearts pounding, they reached the balcony doors.

Emily found it strange that such a tiny flat area between the windows on the slanted roof could be called a "balcony". The height and the ancient, tiny iron railing made her hesitate before stepping out. When she did, she was sure to keep her back pressed firmly against the French doors, as far from the edge as she could manage and still be outside. Sarah was right, this view was much better than the one they'd failed to get down on the street level.

The girls exchanged hushed exclamations when they got their first glimpse of the destruction. A gaping, rugged hole the width of three lanes of traffic and just as long exposed a variety of decrepit pipes, old granite cobblestones, layers of red clay soil, and tons of what looked like snapped boards and planks. In the middle of this strange time capsule beneath the city street was Mr. Hinson's red Ford Explorer, its driver-side door pointing at the cloudless autumn sky. A few yards away was another car that looked an awful lot like the old clunker that belonged to Jason, the college student that rented the basement apartment at the corner next to Mr. Hinson. It was hard to tell, though, because the car was completely upside down.

"Whoa... How could that even happen?" Emily asked.

"I have no idea," Sarah replied. "Maybe it was just bad luck."

"My dad says it was karma. You know, like they did something bad and this is what they get for it," Vivian said.

"Well, your dad just doesn't like Mr. Hinson because he works for the Mayor's office and wouldn't get the taxes on your house lowered," Sarah laughed. "What exactly does he think Jason did to deserve his car ending up like a dead bug in that hole?"

Vivian didn't answer, she just wrinkled up her nose and tilted her head in defeat. Sarah raised her eyebrows as a sign of triumph and then began snapping photos of the wreckage. City workers in coveralls and hardhats peeked out over the broken asphalt from inside the hole every now and then and shouted status reports to other city workers in clean, button-up shirts and slacks who were holding clipboards and looking concerned. Firefighters sat on the bumpers of their huge trucks and laughed and talked with each other and the police who had come to help manage the crowd. The pounding sound of a news helicopter began beating overhead just as two news vans topped with a variety of weird antennae and satellite dishes pulled up and parked beside the fire trucks.

The girls watched as news anchors and camera operators hopped out of the vans and pulled out huge loops of cables and computer gear in preparation for a live broadcast. A female anchor from Channel 6 was applying lipstick in the side mirror of her team's vehicle while the male anchor from Channel 12 appeared to have some kind of temper tantrum about his tie. After exchanging a few words with the police on the scene, both crews scrambled to their posts and extended the enormous antennae on the tops of the vans.

"Quick! Let's get down there and see if we can squeeze into the background. We could be on TV!" Vivian said. Before anyone had time to respond, she ran back into the house and started downstairs. Emily and Sarah followed, but didn't catch up to Vivian until she was slowed down by the crowd on the front sidewalk. They followed Vivian's bright red hair like a beacon in a storm as she pushed her way through to the caution tape at the front of the group. She had managed to squirm her way to a spot only ten feet away from the back of the Channel 12 news anchor who had a camera pointed right on him.

Vivian waved excitedly while Emily and Sarah stood like deer in the headlights, both wondering how they agreed to go along with this plan. Vivian elbowed Emily in the ribs and said through clenched teeth and smiling lips, "Are you two going to make the most of this or what?" Emily let the corners of her mouth curl up, but not without much effort. Sarah smiled nervously and gave a hesitant wave to the camera.

Emily strained to hear what the news anchor was saying, but it was nearly impossible with him facing the opposite direction. She thought she heard the words "hazmat" and "FEMA", both of which she knew meant serious business. Serious and *bad* business.

CHAPTER 2

The three girls stayed at the front lines of the crowd long after the news crews had packed up and moved their vans to a side street. Emily assumed they must be hanging around until Noon to give another live update. The neighbors that had been pressed in tightly around them two hours ago had given up their posts to get kids off to school and themselves off to work. Only a dozen or so remained, including Emily, Sarah, and Vivian.

"Vivi! Come on, we need to get you to school!" her mother called. "I've already called and told them you'd be late thanks to this mess."

"Sarah, please tell me you'll take pictures if anything exciting happens while I'm gone," Vivian whined. "You two are so lucky you get to stay around."

"Well, we can't stay all day—we have lessons at home. I'll get whatever I can with my camera, though," Sarah said.

"Cool! I'll call you tonight," Vivian said over her shoulder as she crossed the street and headed back to her front porch.

"Is this the payment for using her balcony?" Emily whispered to Sarah with a snicker. Sarah was about to reply when her words were cut off with the sudden roar and rumble of the fire truck engine just a few yards away. Both girls backed up and waved exhaust fumes from their faces while the two trucks slowly crept away from the pit and started their return trips to the station. Several police vehicles were soon to follow, leaving only one patrol car and two officers to manage the scene.

"I guess there's nothing left but a mess," Sarah said.

"Maybe. I don't know, I have a weird feeling about this," Emily said while looking off in the distance at nothing in particular.

"Ugh! Not *that* again! You get a weird feeling about *everything*. Come on, we should get back home before our moms decide to send a search party."

They walked west down sidewalks turned into funhouse floors by hundred-year-old tree roots making themselves comfortable. Each girl was lost in her own imagination, coming up with all sorts of mystical reasons the street decided to quit, and neither spoke until they reached the alley their houses shared.

"Hey, call me when you're done and we'll go back down there and see what we can find out from any workers that are still around," Sarah said with a wave as Emily entered her back gate. Emily simply nodded in response, her mind heavy with possibilities.

She settled down in the dining room, her mother's schooling spot of choice this year, and went through her math practice in a fog. Her mom joined her and went through the day's history, science, and vocabulary lessons. After about two hours, she said, "Why do I get the feeling that you're not really paying attention today?"

"What? Oh, sorry. I was just thinking about that sinkhole. We got a good look at it from the balcony on Vivian's house, and it was a lot worse than it looked on the news. Do you think it really just fell in because of too much rain?" Emily said.

"I don't know. I guess it seems like a possible explanation. I don't think the City would need to make up a reason like that," her mom answered.

"You're right. I just got a weird feeling about it is all."

"Well, you know you're feelings about things have been pretty accurate in the past, maybe you should trust your instincts about this, too," said Mom.

Emily didn't respond, instead she let her mother's words sink in and decided to investigate the situation a little more. Sarah was already geared up to start interviewing City workers after lessons today, so the wheels of the plan were already in motion.

She made an effort to focus on the rest of her schoolwork and finished up around one o'clock. After eating a cheese sandwich her mom made her and stuffing a pack of crackers in the pocket of her hoodie, Emily called Sarah. The two agreed to meet at the sidewalk by the alley in ten minutes with an assortment of supplies and a backpack.

They were on a mission.

Emily grabbed a bag and crammed in her dad's tape recorder, a notebook and pen, the mini digital camera she'd gotten in her Christmas stocking last year, some extra batteries, and a bottle of water. She was strangely reminded of a Nancy Drew novel she'd read and let out a little giggle in anticipation of what she and Sarah were about to do. Her thoughts went back to detective stories for a moment and she decided to dig out her plastic magnifying glass and a flashlight just for good measure. "Better to have it and not need it than to need it and not have it," she said to herself. That was her dad's favorite saying and he couldn't let a week go by without reminding at least one family member of it.

She said quick goodbyes to her mother as she raced out the back door and towards the meeting point. Sarah was already there, and Emily could tell from her restlessness that she'd been there for a few minutes. "Quick! My dad just came home for lunch and said there was only one City truck down there by the hole when he drove past," Sarah said. The girls jogged most of the way through the old row houses and slowed to a casual stroll as they rounded the corner nearest the sinkhole as not to look desperate. Emily half expected Sarah to put her hands in her pockets and start whistling like she hadn't even noticed the gaping wound in the road, her act was so stiff and artificial.

Just as the scene came into full view, they saw two men in hardhats climb into a white truck with a stylized image of the James River, the City's logo, on the side. They sat there for a moment, sparking both girls' curiosity, then started the truck and headed west down Franklin Street. "I bet they're going to The Market for lunch," Emily said. "I see those trucks there all the time."

"Now's our chance, let's go over where there's no yellow tape and get a closer look! If we get busted, we can just say we came up from the hillside and didn't notice we were in an off-limits area," Sarah said. She grabbed Emily by the elbow and pulled her across the street with long strides. They rounded the traffic circle, a loop of road around a tiny island of grass that was there only so people could enjoy the hillside view of the city's historic Shockoe Bottom. Now the grass island was nowhere to be seen, and the roadway looked like it had been hit by a meteorite. Sarah stopped near a giant oak tree that sat only about five feet from the broken asphalt. Its roots splayed in all directions and jutted over the darkness of the hole. The sight reminded Emily of her little brother's hair first thing in the morning, only much more surreal.

Sarah dug into her backpack and pulled out the camera she had used earlier that morning. She crept closer to the edge of the hole, wrapped the camera's neck strap around her wrist, and stretched her arms out in front of her to get a better shot. Sarah snapped five or six pictures and moved to the other side of the tree's trunk to get a different angle. Emily could tell that she was focusing more on getting a good photo than she was on her own safety. "Uh, be careful... The asphalt over there doesn't have much soil under it," Emily warned.

Before Sarah could even answer, the piece of road on which she was standing took a sickening dip towards the hole. Huge clumps of mud fell off of the oak's roots as a result of the jostling and made no sound of hitting the bottom. Sarah leapt back onto the sidewalk and panted. "Holy *cats*," she gasped. "I couldn't even see the bottom from there. The other side has some clay and rock sticking out like a shelf, but over here it's just straight down."

Emily turned and picked up a few fat acorns off the ground. She leaned towards the sinkhole, careful to keep her feet on the sidewalk, and tossed one in. Nothing. She tilted her head at an angle and aimed her ear to catch the sound as she tossed in another. After several seconds, she thought she heard a light tap. Emily repeated the last toss, ear at the ready. One, two, three, four, pop! The acorns were either hitting rock at the base of the hole or were bouncing off of something on their way down and she never even heard it hit bottom. She hoped it was the former. "Oooh..."

"I know! This is some seriously weird stuff! Did you notice something *missing*?" Sarah said. Emily thought about it for a bit, but was so bothered by the whole bizarre event that she couldn't place what was out of place. Her puzzled expression served as her answer. Sarah filled in the blank for her, "The smell. There's nothing—no gas, no sewage, no nothing. With all of those pipes and stuff, you'd think there should be *something* stinky, right? It just smells like my Grandma's basement."

"Okay, there is some seriously weird stuff going on here. That's no 'water pocket', either," Emily said. "I told you I had a feeling about this."

Just as Sarah opened her mouth to respond with a snide comment, the white pickup pulled up to its opening in the yellow tape. The girls ducked behind the old oak and tried desperately to think of how to get away unseen. Both doors on the truck opened and closed, and Emily head the men talking about lunch as their conversation moved and settled only a few feet away.

CHAPTER 3

Emily and Sarah held their breath and pressed their backs into the bark of the old oak, attempting to make themselves as narrow and tree-like as possible. The workmen were just on the other side of the tree.

"I never thought I'd get so sick of just sitting around on the job. Most of the time that's what I'm hoping to do," one man said with a laugh.

"I'm right with you. I'd rather be down in there writing work orders or getting some of those pipes fitted, but the boss says just stay out. Watch the site and make sure nothing happens." Emily wondered what else their boss feared *could* happen. Was there a chance it could get worse?

She was considering a number of grim and destructive possibilities when she felt Sarah tugging at her sleeve. Emily saw her pointing to the grass at the edge of the sidewalk opposite the tree from where the City workers were standing. Sarah then gave a tiny gesture with her index finger showing that she intended them to go down the hill. The grassy area dropped off to a steep slope that reached the winding park road about forty feet down. Emily had no desire to go sliding down that hill, but could see no alternative escape route. She gave Sarah a nod, and Sarah replied with counting off on her fingers: one, two, three!

The girls ducked over and ran to the hillside in three long, stealthy strides. When they reached the grass, both instinctively turned to make the decent walking sideways. They fought their own momentum and managed to make it to the park road without rolling down and breaking any bones. Emily leaned over and held her knees, trying to catch her breath. This was not the kind of excitement she'd planned for the afternoon, and Sarah's expression showed that she felt the same way.

"Did you hear that?" Sarah pointed uphill and panted.

"Yeah, that doesn't sound good," Emily replied. "I don't think this is anything like what we thought it was this morning." Her mind went back to all of the reasons the workers could have been told not to work, and her imagination spiraled out of control. "What if the whole neighborhood is about to get sucked down and they just don't want anyone to panic?"

"There's no way the city would keep something like that quiet, they'd tell everyone so we could evacuate and no one would get hurt," Sarah said. A long pause after her reply made Emily think that Sarah might just have been considering the idea a bit more carefully. Her eyebrows pinched together and a furrow appeared on her forehead. "Come on, let's get back to our block and find out what the latest word is on the news."

The girls followed the curving park road to a steep set of stairs that ascended the hill and met the sidewalk a block west of the sinkhole. The two workmen sat in the tailgate of their truck, overlooking the enormous pit, and ate lunch. After a glance toward the surreal scene, Emily and Sarah jogged toward their alley and tried to burn off some of the adrenaline they had pumped up in the last few minutes. Emily's heart and mind where still racing when they turned onto 28th Street and slowed their feet. "Come on, we can go use my computer and check the headlines. There's nothing on TV news for at least another hour," she said to Sarah.

Emily's mother was in the kitchen chopping vegetables when the girls burst in the back door. They tried to act normal, but it only came across as stiff and awkward. "Hey! Did you two find out anything cool this afternoon?" Mom asked.

"No, not really," Emily said. "We're going to go check the news sites and see what the story is. We didn't really have anyone to talk to down there."

"No one would talk to you?"

"Uh, there was no one there to talk," Emily answered.

"Well, that's awfully strange," Mom said with a worried look. "I thought for sure the Department of Public Works would have someone down there at least trying to reconnect the gas. The whole block between 30th and 31st is going to have to find another way to make dinner tonight and most will be without hot water until something is done." She looked lost in thought, so Emily and Sarah gave a quick wave and wound through the living room toward the stairs.

Emily's room was on the third floor. It had slanted walls made by the slope of the roof which gave the space a cozy, cave-like feeling. The dormer windows on the front of the house created two nooks which had cushioned benches tucked in them and a peppering of stuffed animals. At the end farthest from the door sat Emily's desk and computer. The girls dropped their backpacks in the middle of the floor and hurried to switch on the machine. Emily flopped into the desk chair and Sarah pulled up a beanbag and sunk in.

A few long minutes passed before the computer was fully awake. Emily directed it toward the Channel 12 News website to see what was given as the "official" story of the sinkhole. It was there on the first page—an aerial photo of the scene. They could make out the crowds still pressed in around the yellow tape, so it must have been from that morning. With Mr. Hinson's truck on its side in the hole, it looked like it was resting on its wheels in the mouth of a cave in the photo shot from above. Jason's car, however, looked worse belly-up.

She read aloud to Sarah, "City officials fear the sewage leak and severed gas lines have created an unhealthy environment and warn residents to stay at least fifty feet from the opening. Randall White, Department of Public Works Director, advises that the natural gas lines should be reconnected within a few days, but the sewers have been blocked and rerouted until repairs can be made."

"So why didn't anything stink?" Sarah asked. "We were right there on top of that thing and I sure didn't smell any gas or sewage, did you?"

"No, but maybe the gas is heavier than air and sank to the bottom of the hole. I don't know about the sewers. Maybe they shut the valves before a lot got out. I don't guess a lot of people were flushing toilets and stuff that early in the morning. I mean, it was *technically* still night," Emily said.

"Right, but do you remember when that hurricane came through two years ago and dumped all the rain that flooded the playground and backed up the sewers? You could smell that at least six or seven blocks away."

Emily nodded slowly, suspicions about the sinkhole growing by the second. "I have an idea."

The girls borrowed a small video camera that belonged to Emily's mother, using the excuse that they wanted to make a news show about the neighborhood's latest attraction. Using some Velcro straps and a few feet of masking tape just for good measure, they attached a bright flashlight to the side of the camera. Out in the garage, which Emily only dared enter in extreme circumstances because of the dust and spiders, they found a 5-gallon bucket of heavy-duty nylon string that her dad used to pull wires through walls when he was running computer networking cable for work. The bucket was made to be used as a dispenser, with the end of the string coming through a little hole in the lid, so they decided to take the whole thing. Judging by the layer of dust on the lid, he wouldn't miss it before they brought it back.

Though the nylon string was slippery and difficult to work with, Emily used some of the knot-tying skills her mom had taught her when she studied macramé for art class and made a small net to wrap around the camera and flashlight creation. Sarah added a little more masking tape so the camera wouldn't tip over or fall out of its new hammock. Emily attached the end of the string from the bucket to the top of the net with a few solid knots pulled it extra-tight. She gave the line a few yanks and watched the camera and flashlight bob up and down, satisfied that they were well attached.

"We should try and go back right after dinner, like around six-thirty or seven o'clock," Emily said. "It starts getting dark now by seven, so we should at least have some shadows."

"Okay, I'll tell my mom we're going to be here working on the scrapbook and you can tell your mom you're at my house," Sarah added.

Emily didn't want to lie to her parents, but she knew there was no way they'd allow her to go three blocks away without an adult after dark. Besides, this was serious. Sarah left and Emily helped her mother set the table for dinner. She asked about going to Sarah's as they were finishing up dessert, and her parents said it was okay with them as long as it was okay with Sarah's parents. "Just be home by eight!" her mother shouted to her from the dining table as she was already climbing the stairs.

In her room, Emily realized she had forgotten to plan one critical part of the operation—how to get the camera and huge bucket of string out of the house without making her parents suspicious. Looking around frantically for some kind of answer, she spotted a big paper shopping bag her grandmother had given her because Emily had commented on the colorful graphics printed on the sides. "Way to go, Grandma!" she whispered. Emily laid the bucket on its side in the bottom of the bag and nestled the camera into the small bit of empty space beside it. On top, she added a couple of skeins of yarn, a spiral notebook, and a thick bundle of tissue paper that she had squirreled away from gifts past. Collecting the shopping bag, she headed for the back door.

"Wow! You two must be planning to do a *lot* of work on that scrapbook this evening," her dad said as he eyed the bag in her hand.

"Yeah, well, the hole in the road is kind of a big deal," she replied, trying to sound casual.

"That it is," he said. "Remember your manners."

Emily found Sarah waiting for her by the neighbor's privacy fence outside the back gate. The two of them slinked off to the sinkhole for the third time that day, confident that they would get to the bottom of it in more ways than one.

CHAPTER 4

The girls set up their base of operations behind the old oak tree that had saved them from trouble once already. Both felt more comfortable knowing they could make a quick getaway down the hillside if push came to shove.

Since this was the side of the sinkhole that dropped right off into nothing, unlike the other side which not only had rocky outcroppings, but two cars in the way, Emily thought it would be the best place to lower the camera. "We'll have to go to the left of the tree for a ways to get the camera clear of the roots. My mom will *kill* me if anything happens to it," she said.

The evening had turned violet and the sun had just dipped below the horizon. The old gaslights that lined the streets in Church Hill glowed in the distance, but, much to the girls' satisfaction, the broken gas lines had left this block and the next dark. They tiptoed away from the oak with the bucket of string and the tiny camera and settled on the edge of the sidewalk just out of range from the tree's tangled roots. Crouched beside the dark pit, Emily switched on the flashlight and the camera, pressed the record button, and then stretched to carefully lower it over the edge of the broken asphalt. "Okay, go."

Sarah, who had been holding tightly to the line coming out of the bucket's lid, began to let the string feed out a foot or two at a time. The weight of the little video recorder pulled the string taught as it slowly dropped into the abyss. The two girls watched in awe as what seemed like endless lengths of the nylon line were fed into the hole. A few minutes later, the string relaxed—the camera had come to rest on something. The girls hoped it was at the bottom and *not* underwater. There was no way Emily could explain that one to her mother. "Let's pull it up a little bit and just let it hang there for a while before we take it back out," she said. Sarah reeled in two arm-lengths of line and guided them back into the bucket.

Two minutes passed that felt like hours. Teaming up for the camera's removal, Emily pulled up the line as Sarah frantically tucked them back into the container. Just as her arms were starting to cramp from the repetitive motions, Emily saw the glow from the flashlight bounce off of Jason's car at the other edge of the hole. She reached as far as she could without leaving the sidewalk, fearing she would not be spared the fall like Sarah had been that afternoon, and gently lifted the camera over the edge. Emily breathed a huge sigh of relief when she discovered it was dry and unharmed, and then she switched off the recording.

"Awesome!" Sarah whispered. "I can't wait to see what it got!" They gathered their gear and ducked back behind the oak, brushing acorns and fallen leaves out of the way to sit down. Emily wrestled the camera out of its string and tape bonds and fumbled to get the flashlight free so they could open the tiny screen and take a peek at the machine's voyage. The camera showed that it had recorded eighteen minutes in total. They rewound the tape and huddled close to the glow of the screen to see what it would reveal.

The girls watched as the camera, shaky in Emily's hand, went over the asphalt. The shaking stopped, but the slow turning began. Sarah fought motion sickness and Emily struggled to tell in which direction the camera was pointing. It was easy at first, but after it passed the overturned cars and giant chunks of granite, it all looked pretty much the same. There were broken pipes that looked like they must have been at least a hundred years old, lots of split planks and logs near those, and what looked like a big wooden box that was pinched off at one end and dripped with water. "Look! That's an old wooden sewer line. My dad says most of them have been under this neighborhood since the 1870s," Emily said.

They could see where the walls of that side of the hole looked damp, but there was certainly no visible sewage mess. The camera dropped farther and farther, showing layers of black soil and bright red clay in the flashlight's circle. Some stones colored orange by the clay soon appeared, followed shortly after by more granite. Either Emily's eyes were playing tricks on her, or these hunks of granite weren't just hunks—they were huge blocks. As her logical mind was trying to make sense of what she had seen, the camera abruptly hit bottom and tipped to one side.

The girls waited impatiently for the rig to ascend again, pressing closer to the view screen. The camera popped upright, rose a few feet, and turned slowly to pan the bottom of the shaft. The bright beam of the flashlight caught all sorts of sparkles from the pebbles in the muddy walls as it surveyed. Then they saw it.

For just a few seconds as the camera twirled, Emily and Sarah could see the opening of a huge stone tunnel. Judging by how much it filled the screen, it had to be at least six or seven feet high, and there was no way its arched top was a natural formation of the granite. "No way," Emily said as she heard Sarah gasp. The camera continued its slow circle around the shaft and the girls watched eagerly for the tunnel to come back into view. The flashlight had just barely illuminated the opening in the stone when it started to rise once more. A quick glow of something yellow flicked on the screen as the camera climbed up and away from the bottom.

"Did you see that? Something was *in* there!" Sarah exclaimed. "And don't tell me it was a rat—it was big."

"We should watch it on the TV, that way we can see everything better," Emily said. There was no way she'd argue with Sarah that what they'd seen was a rat. She had noticed, too, that whatever was in there was as large as the tunnel was tall. Her bad feeling about the sinkhole had returned, and this time is was a lot more nagging than before.

CHAPTER 5

After returning to their block, Emily and Sarah decided there was no way they could watch the video they had captured on a television at either house without blowing their cover story for the night. Sarah ran down the alley to her back gate and she and Emily disappeared inside their houses.

Emily dodged as much conversation with her parents as she could—she was a terrible liar and her mother could always tell when something was up. She tucked the shopping bag that concealed the camera and string in the corner behind her laundry hamper and collapsed onto the bed. Emily felt like she had been awake for days, but her mind was still busy with all of the evening's adrenaline and the recollections of what she had seen in the video. Her body felt too heavy to move, and without even changing into pajamas, she drifted off to sleep.

Everything was suddenly cool and damp, and Emily noticed she was in complete darkness. Her hands searched for any sign of where she might be and for anything that could help her see. She hesitated and took a few tiny steps forward with her arms extended and her hands feeling for obstacles and clues. The floor was not completely flat, and a bump caught her sneaker and threw her balance off enough to send her stumbling. A cold, wet wall stopped her, and had she not had her hands at the ready, would have hit face-first.

She decided to keep her hands on the wall and move to her right. Emily moved her feet much more carefully and noticed the lumpy floor started to angle sharply downhill. She had shuffled along for several minutes, which in her dream-mind felt like both years and seconds at the same time, when she heard a voice far in the distance. "Hello?" she called. "Can anyone help me?" She stayed perfectly still and listened as hard as she could for a response, but all she could hear was the faint dripping of water from somewhere in front of her. "Hello?" she tried again, louder this time.

Her ears picked up on a rhythmic squeaking and a hollow *thud-thud-thud* that seemed to be getting closer. "Can you hear me?" Emily shouted. "I'm lost, help!" A dull, flickering orange glow began to illuminate what she discovered to be a long corridor. The light slowly approached the curve that had obscured its source from her view and Emily noticed the corridor was made of some kind of stone. Thoughts began popping in her head like firecrackers and she felt a sense of panic stirring in her stomach. She held her breath as the light came closer. It was an oil lantern, the old fashioned type like she'd seen in photos of her great grandfather when he worked for the railroad, and it was in the hand of a large homeless man in a long overcoat and a hood. He was pulling a rusty little red wagon behind him with a frayed rope tied to the handle so he could tow it without having to bend down. It was filled with a heap of mismatched shoes.

Emily guessed he must have been at least as tall as a professional basketball player because he had to duck his head to avoid the high but irregular ceilings. He was mumbling to himself and was in some kind of argument with no one in particular about work boots when he stopped a few yards away from her in surprise. "Heh! What are ya' doin' in here?" he growled.

"I don't know, I just opened my eyes and I was here in the dark. Can you tell me how to get out?" Emily said.

"Out?" he asked as he stepped closer to her and leaned suspiciously to get a better look in the light of his lantern. An odd, musky smell filled her nostrils. When the light moved between them, Emily saw what was under the hood. The man had dark skin and short, course hair like a pig's all over his face, neck, and hands. Protruding from between his lips were two huge teeth that looked more like tusks. They pointed upwards and stopped just below his wide, upturned nose. His eyes seemed to glow with a strange yellow spark. He looked like just like a boar.

Emily took a step back away from him in shock and caught her heel on the rough floor. She fell backwards and, just before she landed square on her bottom, awoke with a start. She was in her room, the lights were still on and she realized she had been dreaming. The clock on the wall above her desk showed it was just after three o'clock in the morning.

CHAPTER 6

Emily felt like a zombie at the kitchen table for breakfast. Her mother was concerned that she'd fallen asleep in her clothes and asked at least five times if Emily suspected she might be coming down with something. The truth was she couldn't get back to sleep after that dream. Everything in it felt so real, the cold stone walls, the fumbling in the dark, even the *smell* she noticed when the strange pig-man leaned towards her. She suspected yesterday's events had just put too much of a strain on her subconscious and these little tangents her mind had gone off on had formed one bizarre display of her imagination while she was sleeping.

She stretched and tried to find the energy to chew. Emily knew she was going to need to muster all of the focus she could for her lessons of the day, or Mom was going to kill any request she made to see Sarah in the afternoon. As an emergency tactic, Emily dragged herself to the coffee pot and made herself a cup. "Wow. That bad, huh?" her mother asked.

"I just didn't sleep well. Weird dreams and all," Emily said.

"All right then, let's just keep it at *one* cup, okay? You know that stuff stunts your growth." Mom said with a wink.

Emily's brother, Max, stomped downstairs and poured himself a bowl of cereal. His brow furrowed when he saw the circles under her eyes and the coffee cup in her hand. He was only seven years old, so a shortage of sleep was virtually unknown to him. "You look like crap," he smiled.

"All right, Max, that's no way to start the day," their mother said. "You had it easy spending the day with Jeremy's family yesterday at the Nature Center while Emily took care of her school work *and* did some investigative reporting down at the sinkhole with Sarah. She has good reasons for being tired, which I'm sure you'll find out after you catch up on *your* lessons today." Max pouted for a moment, and when Mom's back was turned, shot an ugly glare at Emily. "Speaking of reporting, what did you girls find out?"

"Oh, uh, we... got some really cool pictures and, um, heard some workers talking about this and that. Not really anything good. We wanted to, uh, get the photos in the scrapbook so we can keep an eye on the repairs as they go," Emily said. She was far too tired to lie convincingly, so she kept the conversation a mix of fact and fiction to throw her mother off the scent. Mom nodded and shifted her concentration to finishing her breakfast while going over the lesson plans for the rest of the week.

Emily's mind trailed off and images from the video camera's tiny preview screen floated through her thoughts. She wasn't so sure if, after last night's dream, she really wanted to take a closer look at that tape. Sarah would be set on it, though. Talking Sarah out of *anything* she had set in her mind was like trying to teach bricks to fly.

Lessons weren't so painful. Emily suspected her mother was taking it easy on her because the majority of her work for the day involved review and reading. Her brother, however, had lots of catching up to do and was taking most of Mom's attention. To Emily, this was a good thing. She finished early and was making herself lunch when Sarah called.

"Hey, are you done yet?" she asked Emily.

"Yeah, I finished up about an hour ago. Why?" Emily knew the answer, she was just hoping to act indifferent to diffuse Sarah's excitement a little.

"What do you mean *why*? We still need to watch that video on a television and find out what the heck that was!" Sarah said in a hushed tone. "When can you come over? We can use the TV in my dad's den while he's at work."

"Give me about fifteen minutes," Emily replied.

She tried to drag out lunch as much as she had breakfast. She was in no hurry to find out if her bad dream had any kind of roots in reality, but Max came tearing into the kitchen for his lunch break and made Emily realize there were worse things to endure—little brothers.

Sarah plugged the video camera into the enormous television that filled almost one whole wall in her father's den. Emily pressed rewind and they waited for the buzzing motor to stop, signaling that it was time to watch carefully and take notes. The video began and the two girls stared wide-eyed at the screen, Sarah on the edge of her seat with excitement and Emily terrified. She decided it was best to keep her dream secret instead of hearing Sarah go on and on about her "bad feelings."

The tension built as the television showed the camera on its long journey down into the hole. When it hit the bottom, Emily readied her finger over the pause button. She hoped to freeze whatever it was they had seen the night before on the screen to get a better look. "There! Stop!" Sarah blurted. The girls leaned in and squinted to study the strange yellow sparkle in the tunnel opening. "Is that what I think it is?" asked Sarah.

Emily could only stare. Her mouth fell open and goosebumps crawled across her skin. There, on the television, were two eyes. They shone in the flashlight's beam like a deer's eyes by the side of the road in car headlights. Whatever they belonged to was far enough back into the tunnel that it was undetectable except for that eerie yellow reflection. "It's... *eyes*." Emily fought the urge to scream as the panic swelled in her.

"*Big* ones," Sarah added. The two stared at the television for a long time. "I guess that weird feeling you were talking about was with good reason."

"What do we do now? Should we tell someone?" Emily asked. They considered their options carefully. If they brought the video to their parents, they'd have to come clean about their actions from the night before. If they showed the video to anyone else, they would probably face a ton of questions and scrutiny. Both girls had practice dealing with the punishments laid down by their parents, but other authorities were completely foreign and intimidating by comparison. The decision was made—they'd fess up.

"Okay, so who goes first?" Sarah asked with a sideways glance at Emily. "You know, your mom is kinda into weird stuff like ghosts and whatever. I bet she'd know what to do next. She might even be so into it that she goes easy on you when she finds out we weren't working on the scrapbook last night." Emily couldn't argue—Sarah was making valid points. She didn't have time to reply before Sarah unhooked the video camera, grabbed the cables, and pulled Emily by the wrist. "Come on! I'll go and back you up."

Mom and Max were still at the dining room table working on science lessons when Emily and Sarah burst in. Emily's palms were sweating and her heart felt as though it was trying to escape through her throat. Her mother shot an annoyed look at her for the disturbance, but it quickly changed to concern when she saw the look on the girls' faces. "What's wrong?"

"We need to show you something," Sarah answered.

"Yeah, on the television. It's important," Emily said.

All four of them went into the living room and Emily and Sarah worked together to cue up the tape. Emily decided she had better start explaining before her mother figured out things on her own once the video started. "Okay... Mom, I'm really sorry, but Sarah and I didn't work on the scrapbook last night." Her mother's face began to pinch and her eyes narrowed, but she didn't say a word. Max looked delighted and hoped to see his sister get in deep trouble. "We wanted to find out more about that sinkhole because we heard the workmen say something about being told *not* to work on it yesterday, just to watch it in case anything happened. We came up with the idea of using the camera and some of dad's cable pulling string to see what was down there, so we went back when it got dark to try it out." Mom had a strange expression that Emily didn't quite understand—a smile was forming at the corners of her mouth.

"Um-hmm, I figured something was going on, but I wasn't sure what," her mother said. "I should have known you were too curious to leave it alone. I would have done the same thing had I heard a comment like that from the work crew. Still, you should have said something to me about this yesterday instead of risking life and limb to get so close to that hole, it's just not stable."

"We found that out," Sarah mumbled.

Emily cut in, "Anyway, we saw something on the tape that is weirder than what those guys were talking about yesterday and we thought you should see it, too." She started the video at the beginning so her mother would get an idea of exactly how deep that sinkhole really was. Mom leaned forward on the couch and studied the camera's trip with obvious fascination. "The part we want you to see is not long after it makes it to the bottom." A few moments passed and Emily paused the tape, capturing the same image she and Sarah had gawked at earlier.

"Whoa! It's a monster!" Max shouted, bounding off of the couch to get a closer look at the TV. The comment made Emily shudder, and even Sarah was visibly upset, a rare thing for someone with her disposition.

"Now, Max, I doubt it's a monster," Mom said, unable to hide her uncertainty. "It is definitely *something*, though. How much more of this did you film?"

"Only a couple of seconds before we starting pulling up the camera," Emily answered.

Her mother thought about it for a minute and said, "There's no denying that there is a tunnel down there. Maybe it was something blown out by the railroad when they put the train tunnel through Church Hill in the 1800s. I guess that's possible. But, uh, the other thing... I don't know."

Mom was distracted then by the telephone ringing in the kitchen. When she left the room to answer it, Max let all the wild images of his imagination out in words. "Ooh! I bet it's the ghost of the train conductor that got buried in the hill when the tunnel collapsed! Or maybe it's a giant, mutated muskrat that came from the riverfront!"

"Don't be an idiot," Emily replied. Sarah snickered, but secretly wondered if the kid was on to something. The three then noticed bits of Mom's conversation from the next room.

"You're kidding me? I doubt that's any kind of coincidence. No, but I think there's a video here you should take a look at. Do you remember me telling you about the crazy stories my grandmother used to tell me about growing up on Venable Street? Well, I'm beginning to think they may not have been so crazy. No, you really just have to see it. Okay. That sounds like a good idea." She said some things in a whisper after that that no one caught, hung up the phone, and came back to the living room. "You're not going to believe this, but your dad just heard on the news that there's another sinkhole. It just showed up in Bryan Park."

CHAPTER 7

Emily remembered going to Bryan Park for a food festival once. On the north side of Richmond, the park was full of old fountains, curvy roads, and azalea bushes that had gone feral. It used to be a popular place for Sunday drives when her grandparents were young, but now it just looked sad and a little neglected.

Mom turned on the television just in time to catch the Noon news wrapping up and showing a "live on the scene" image of the sinkhole, much larger than the one in their neighborhood, which had swallowed up three side-by-side basketball courts. Below the cracked and broken blacktop were thick layers of clay soil and more splintered and broken boards of some type. The reporter looked confused and was clearly relaying some sort of script he was given. "City officials want to emphasize that the latest sinkhole is *not* cause to worry. Heavy rains last month have created pockets of water in areas that were back-filled to improve drainage between the 1940s and the

1960s. These areas are predominantly in parks and on roadways once known for flooding. Homes should not be disturbed by any of these shifts," he read.

Everyone in the living room, even Max, looked at the screen with suspicion. The sinkhole looked completely dry, just like the one a few blocks away. If there had been some huge pocket of water underground, where did it all go? Emily remembered when sinkholes started appearing in yards out in the far end of the neighboring county, but the homes there had been built on top of old coal mines and the structures that once supported the shafts and all of the dirt they'd pack in to fill them had just settled over time. Maybe these holes were something like that, she wondered. She asked her mother about it, but her reply made so much sense that Emily scrapped the idea the two situations were similar, "Those were tiny holes that resulted from pretty large shaft collapses. These are *pits* showing up where no mines ever existed."

Mom called off the rest of Max's lessons for the day and he squealed in celebration. She made them all some popcorn and they spent the rest of the afternoon talking about all of the things that could have *really* caused Richmond's sinkhole problem. No possibility was too wild or extreme, especially considering what they had seen on Emily and Sarah's video.

Around five o'clock, mom reheated some leftovers for dinner. Sarah left to have dinner with her family and decided not to let them in on the previous night's adventure until she knew a little more about what was going on. Dad came home shortly after Sarah left, and they all settled in around the kitchen table. Mom began explaining to Dad about how Emily and Sarah had returned to the hole in the neighborhood last night to send a camera down. It was clear that he was disappointed in the girls for lying about where they were and what they were doing, but he wore the same look of amusement Mom had when she first heard the story. Emily suspected her parents had probably committed a similar act when they were her age because they hadn't grounded her yet.

Her mother then described the video. Dad, being the level-headed skeptic he had always been, decided that he needed to have a look for himself. He left the table and switched on the TV and video camera still connected in the next room. Through the open archway, Emily saw that he, like Mom, watched the video from the very beginning. When he came to the part where the tunnel was illuminated during the camera's slow rotation, he hit rewind and played over and over, pausing a few times to get a better look. "Hmm," was all he said.

Mom raised her eyebrows and waited for Dad's comments when he returned to the table.

"Well?" she asked.

"Well, those are eyes all right. I think the size might be an illusion, though. There's no way to really tell without something nearby for comparison," Dad said.

"Okay. What about the thing I mentioned on the phone?"

"Come on, you know that's just a story. Your grandma told you all kinds of unbelievable stuff."

"What story?" Emily interrupted.

Mom and Dad exchanged glances, and Mom said, "My grandma grew up in the next neighborhood over, in Union Hill. She used to tell me that all the old neighbors she had as a little girl, remember that was in the early 1900s, used to warn the children not to go into the parks at night. She said the old folks made the kids scared to go out after dark by warning them about the creatures who lived under the streets, that they would sometimes come to the surface if things got tough below and they were hungry." Her mother added a hushed, spooky tone to her voice and continued the story. "Grandma told me she saw one once, when she was ten years old. She and her brother had been the last to leave Jefferson Park after a Sunday afternoon ball game. The sun had just set and the old gaslights hadn't been lit yet. They were nearly at the edge of the park when they noticed someone come up out of a manhole cover in the sidewalk just ahead of them. She said all she really paid attention to were his yellow eyes; they seemed to have a glow about them. Uncle Hank grabbed her by the hand and they ran all the way home!"

Emily felt the same uneasiness returning that she had the first time she watched the video on the TV at Sarah's house. Something about her dream was still nagging at her. Dad broke her thoughts by asking, "Did you two go back over there today?"

She snapped out of her imagination and back to the dinner table. "No, we were here all afternoon. We got a little spooked after we watched that video," Emily said.

"Why don't we clean up here and walk down the block to see if Wallace and Jason's cars were pulled out yet?" Dad said. Emily assumed Wallace was Mr. Hinson, since there were only two vehicles in the hole.

Everyone pitched in and helped with the dinner dishes. When they were done, Emily and Max grabbed their jackets while Mom put on her boots and Dad watched the video again. Emily thought it was strange that the whole family was getting excited about this, especially after thinking her parents would flip out when they found out about her sneaking back over to the hole last night when no one was around. She was certainly glad the outcome of events so far was much better than expected.

They walked together, two by two, the few blocks to what was once the traffic circle. The sun was just about to dip below the horizon and the air was cool and crisp. Temperatures in Virginia during October were always unpredictable, but fortunately this year it had been like a storybook autumn so far. Leaves were scattered about, and the ones that still clung to branches were beautiful shades of amber and gold.

As they turned the corner onto Franklin, Emily noticed Mr. Hinson standing on his front porch talking to a man in a shirt and tie. The man carried some sort of thick notebook, so she assumed he must have been someone from his insurance company there to take a look at what must have sounded like a made-up incident. He handed Mr. Hinson a card and said a few more things before giving him a brief wave and walking down to his car. Mr. Hinson gave Emily's parents a smile and a nod as they passed.

"Everything being taken care of?" her father asked.

"Eventually, I suppose. You know insurance companies. They're not sure yet they can consider this 'an act of God' or whatever it is that gets them moving to pay for repairs," Mr. Hinson replied.

"Good luck with that. How about the gas over here? Any word yet from the City?" Dad said.

"That Randall White, he's full of it if you ask me. Public Works is telling us maybe two or three weeks now. You can't expect folks to take cold showers for that long. And this weather could turn harsh at any time, we might be needing some heat," Mr. Hinson said in disgust.

"Very true. We'll be sure to try and get everyone to contact our councilman and see if he can get Public Works to move things along faster."

"I'd appreciate it. I've got to go make a few calls myself, so you folks have a good night now." He turned and stepped back inside.

Dad, true to his nature, was prepared for the lack of gaslights on the blocks around the sinkhole. He pulled two flashlights from his pants pockets, handed one to Mom, and switched on the one he kept for himself. Panning the bright beam from the powerful lights over the pit, we saw everything just as it had been the day before—lots of broken asphalt and two trashed cars teetering on ledges of granite.

"Here, come around this side, but be careful," Emily said as she led them around the hole to the oak tree on the other side. "This is where Sarah and I stood when we lowered the camera down. It drops off almost straight down on this side without all that stuff sticking out like over there," she said as she pointed to the strange mix of wood and stone jutting from the walls opposite them. Mom did the same thing Emily had done the day before; she picked up a few acorns off the ground and tossed them, one at a time, into the opening and listened for their impact. Dad held on to Max's hand and clearly expected him to try and get a closer look from a spot with unsteady footing.

They stared into the hole for a few minutes, taking in all the details. Emily thought about the story her mother had told them at dinner, the one her grandmother had told her, and began to wonder if standing out there in the dark was such a good idea. That's when she heard the sounds.

Dad and Max had taken a seat on the grass at the edge of the sidewalk and were watching the streetlights flick on in the portion of the city over the river. Mom tilted her head a little and stepped closer to Emily. "Did you just hear that?" she whispered.

"If you mean something moving around down there, then yes."

The two leaned toward the hole, sure to keep their feet on the sidewalk, and pointed their ears in the direction of the sound. Emily heard it again. It sounded like mumbling, two voices in conversation at a great distance. They stopped as abruptly as they began. Mom and Emily looked at each other in disbelief and strained to hear the sounds again. Nothing.

"Maybe it's Public Works? You know this city has lots of really old tunnels that were used as escape routes during the Civil War. I think bootleggers used them during Prohibition, too, to sneak illegal whiskey to people who could pay well. I bet that's what the city is using to check the damage near the bottom end of this hole," Mom tried hard to find a logical explanation for what they had just witnessed. "That might also be the tunnel we saw in your video. I saw the opening for the tunnel under Monumental Church down the hill several years ago, and it was lined with granite and looked similar to this one."

The hairs on Emily's arms stood on end and she felt a suspicious tingling at the back of her neck. She was officially spooked. "Let's just go home. Maybe we can see what's going on at the other sinkhole on the news at ten. Can I stay up and watch it?"

"I suppose so," Mom answered. "Hey, you two! Nothing else to see here, move along," she called to Dad and Max. They strolled home, talking about the neighborhood, Richmond's history, and poor Mr. Hinson's car along the way. Emily was relieved to be safely inside her house and not out on a dark sidewalk where she was certain something evil was lurking and waiting to grab her and take her under the streets.

CHAPTER 8

Emily had another restless night of sleep. She lay awake in bed for well over an hour, images of the latest sinkhole she saw on the news flashing through her mind. Imagination, once her friend and ally, and recently become an enemy. All kinds of wild and crazy scenarios played out on the fringes of her conscious thoughts and left her feeling drained, but unable to rest.

She eventually slipped into a dream. Like the last, it was dark and damp. A few dim lights, more lanterns, hung from rough posts which stood at odd angles. There were dozens of tables and booths piled high with everything from vegetables to household junk and pots and pans. The scene was a strange combination of a farmers' market and a garage sale, but there was no one in sight to tend the wares.

Emily walked through the empty market and strained in the low light to see the specialty displayed at each booth. She noticed she was walking on hard packed dirt, not an interior floor like she had assumed. Butterflies in her stomach began to flutter. Looking around desperately for some kind of sign or other indicator of where she was, she saw a strange latticework of short boards and long planks climbing the walls. The lattice continued over the ceiling, at least twenty feet high, holding back red clay and chunks of granite. Emily was underground.

She jolted up in bed, sweat plastering her fine blonde hair to her neck and forehead. It took a moment before she recognized the faint glow of the streetlamps below through the dormer windows and could tell she was in her room. Emily shuffled to the tiny bathroom just outside her door and splashed some water on her face. She looked terrible—dark circles shadowed her eyes, which were bloodshot and bleary. Her skin was paler than usual. Emily decided then that the events of the past few days had officially been too much to handle.

Instead of climbing back into bed, she sat at her desk and switched on the computer. As she waited for it to boot up, she noticed four-thirty on the clock overhead. The plan was to try and bore herself with her limited internet access and get back into the mood for sleep, but instead, she became completely absorbed in researching other historical accounts of sinkholes in Richmond over the last hundred years or so. There had been about a dozen, and all but one of them had appeared in a park or at an intersection of two roads. The one that stood out as different had shown up in the back yard of then mayor John Fulmer Bright in 1929. Emily did not believe there was any way it could have been a coincidence.

She printed out all of the news accounts she found that were reputable and stacked them in order from oldest to most recent, not counting the two that had just appeared in the past few days. The clock on the wall now read seven-twenty. So much for getting back to sleep, Emily thought.

She showered, dressed, and made it to the breakfast table before Dad left for the day. "You're down early. What's up?" he asked.

"Couldn't sleep. A weird dream woke me up a couple of hours ago and I just stayed up," she passed him the stack of articles she had printed. "I found all of these when I was trying to bore myself back to sleep." Her father leaned back against the kitchen counter and scanned through each page carefully, occasionally making a noise that meant he was either curious or surprised about some detail one contained.

"You found all of this on the internet?" he asked. She nodded. "If you're feeling up to it later, I bet you can find a *lot* more than this down at the State Library. They have just about every newspaper article printed in Virginia since the

1860's cataloged on microfilm. You can have them print off whatever you like. I'll ask your mom if she'll let you and Sarah ride your bikes down there if you want—it's not far at all. If she says yes, she can run it by Sarah's mother."

Emily had been with her mother and Max to the State Library just a few months ago to meet a "Historical Interpreter" who portrayed Thomas Jefferson. She was pleasantly surprised to discover that "Historical Interpreter" just meant that he was an actor in costume. She had a fun time and remembered the librarians there had been much nicer than the ones she saw regularly at the neighborhood branch library. "Sure, it sounds cool," Emily said, always happy for the opportunity to go anywhere on her own, independent of her parents. Riding her bike the two miles along the steep hills between her house and library was a bit daunting, but she'd take that over her mother chauffeuring her around.

Much to her delight, Dad convinced Mom that his plan was a good one. They looked over the articles Emily had put together earlier and whispered about them as they cleaned up the breakfast dishes and packed Dad's lunch. Mom had even agreed to wrap up lessons early enough for Emily to make it to the library before the lunch rush doubled the downtown traffic. She called Sarah's mother and explained to her that the girls had been working on a project together about the sinkholes and how these were no new thing for Richmond. She convinced her to allow Sarah to join Emily for some "hands-on research" in the archives room at the State Library. Emily could only imagine what Sarah would think when she heard the plan. She was pretty sure that Sarah was sharp enough to pick up that *something* was going on that they needed to look into.

Emily hurried though her schoolwork, careful to not let Mom notice how distracted and tired she was, fearing that her mother would put a stop to the bicycle trip. Max was still at the table working on addition practice when Emily went out the backdoor with her backpack.

She pulled her bike out of the shed and grabbed a thick chain lock off a hook on the wall. She hung the lock around her handlebars, letting the bulk of it rest on the bike's frame, and tucked the key into the pocket of her jeans. Sarah rolled up to the back gate just as Emily was closing the shed. "Ready?" she called.

"Let's go!" Emily said, finally perking up from her sleepy morning.

The first half of the trip was easy—it was downhill. They went as far West as they could on Franklin Street and then had to travel over a few blocks to Broad Street to get around the huge, archaic train station that sat right beside the overhead highway. Both girls had to pedal standing up to make it to the other side of the station, and then they gave up and walked their bikes the four remaining uphill blocks to the library.

From Noon until almost four o'clock, the girls scanned though microfilm records on the library computers. They found at least six more reports of sinkholes that Emily didn't come across on the internet, so they printed records of those and several newspaper articles that gave interesting details about the dozen she had already noted. After carefully tucking the thick stack of copies into her backpack, Emily and Sarah signed out of the archives room. They unlocked their bikes from the rack outside and started the trip home before the afternoon traffic really picked up.

As they walked the last steep blocks before their own, Sarah said, "Hey, since it's still light out, why don't we go see if they pulled out those cars yet?" Emily was curious herself and had no reason not to go along with the suggestion. They got back on their bicycles and rode to the hole.

Both vehicles were still in unnatural positions in the mouth of the pit, and there were no City trucks in sight. It looked as though absolutely no progress had been made to do *anything* about the mess in the middle of what was once a nice, normal street.

To get a good look at things, Emily and Sarah went to their preferred spot near the big oak. They leaned their bikes against the tree and peered into the sinkhole. Emily said, "Poor Mr. Hinson told my dad last ni-" but let the statement drop when she spotted something moving under Jason's car. "Look!" she pointed.

"What? I saw that two days ago," Sarah replied.

"No! Something was moving over there, I swear it!"

"Seriously? Maybe it's a squirrel or a rat or something," Sarah said.

"It was *way* bigger than either one. I think someone's in there." Emily held onto Sarah's hand and the two tiptoed off of the curb toward the hole to try and see if maybe it had been an illusion, a trick of the fading light. Sliding slowly closer, they saw something flit through the upside down windows on the car. Both girls startled, and when they did, the hunk of asphalt on which they stood gave a sickening crack.

"Quick, move!" Emily shouted, but it was too late. The road gave way and fell from beneath their feet. They struggled to grab onto the roots of the oak tree as everything seemed to shift into slow motion. Emily saw Sarah a few feet below her, hanging on to a tangle of debris that shifted, snapped, and sent her sliding down the side of the hole, screaming. Before the image could really register, the thin roots Emily had been clinging to began breaking like old strings. She let go with her left hand and reached for a higher grip while trying to dig her toes into the packed soil for support.

Emily took a sharp intake of breath just as the handful of roots in her right hand tore away.

She dropped into the pit after Sarah.

CHAPTER 9

Sarah was either having a panic attack or struggling to reclaim the breath that had been knocked out of her from the rough landing she endured. It was even rougher when Emily landed on top of her. They had slid down the steep wall of the pit, fortunate they did not free-fall the entire distance. Emily's backpack had spared her from the ends of broken boards and stones that protruded from the dirt, while Sarah had taken her mother's advice and worn a thick jacket to the library.

The two patted themselves all over, checking for injuries. Emily did not trust her body to tell her the truth, however, as she feared she was either dreaming or going into some strange state of shock. She noticed Sarah feeling around in her hair for head wounds, "Are you okay?" she panted.

"I think so," Sarah answered. "I thought for sure for a minute that I was dead—until *you* tried to kill me." Emily could always count on Sarah to find the humor in any situation. A laugh broke through Emily's lips and quickly turned into hysterics. She wasn't sure if Sarah's joke had started it or if it just tore down the dam that held back how delighted she was to still be alive after what just happened. Sarah joined in and they laughed until Emily had to wipe tears from her cheeks.

When the gravity of their situation took hold, the moment of joy gave way to one of desperation. "How the heck are we going to get out of here?" Emily asked.

"Maybe if we start yelling, someone will hear us. Someone is sure to notice our bikes and come check it out, right?" Sarah said.

Emily nodded and the girls stood. Pointing their faces towards the fleeting daylight, they called "Help! Down here! Hello!" They shouted until their throats and lungs ached. By then, night had arrived.

Emily remembered that, aside from the addition of the copies she and Sarah made at the library that afternoon, the contents of her backpack were the same as they were two days ago. She wrestled off the pack and dug into it with filthy hands. Emily grabbed her prize, switched it on, and raised it over her head in triumph—a flashlight. Sarah clapped and did a tiny dance of approval. "You don't have a ladder in there, do you?" she laughed.

"I wish," Emily said. "I think we should try something else."

"Like what? That?" Sarah asked, pointing at the tunnel. The look on Emily's face was completely serious. "No! You're kidding, right? No way I'm going in *there*."

"What do you suggest? We climb?" Emily said. "I don't think we have any other choice besides sitting here and *hoping* someone comes in the morning. Do you realize how cold it's been getting at night? Do you realize how many *rats* hang out around this neighborhood after dark? I certainly don't want to try and sleep with a rat family cozying up to me to keep warm!" Emily felt her cheeks go hot. It was not often she asserted herself with Sarah. Sarah was three years older, and as every teenager knows, your rung on the social ladder is directly connected to your age. This time, Emily felt she had to do something or run the risk of a bad situation taking a turn for the worse. "Listen, I have the flashlight and some extra batteries. If we go in the tunnel and find out it ends just a little ways away, we won't have lost anything. If we go in the tunnel and find a way out, we could save our own butts *and* get a few more clues about what's been going on down here. I told you my mom and I heard someone talking down here last night—they *had* to have come through there," Emily said.

Sarah's eyes pointed at the floor and her mouth curved into a grimace. "All right, but you're going first."

The flashlight shone toward the end of the tunnel, only six feet or so away. Sarah grabbed the sleeve of Emily's jacket and they entered the narrow cave on tiptoes. As they approached the end of the tunnel, they noticed a swelling on the wall had concealed a sharp right turn of the corridor.

Emily's stomach was turning and her head felt strangely light. The weird pounding in her ears told her it was nerves that were making her brain turn into some strange primal thing. Every drip of water, every drag of Sarah's shoes, even the light flick of dirt falling down the shaft the two girls had slid down earlier registered in her ears. The old basement smell she had first noticed about the hole days ago faded as she rounded the bend. It was replaced by something different, more like a cross between her mom cooking onions and her brother's dirty laundry.

The tunnel ahead of them went on for at least a city block. There was a slight downward dip at the bottom that made the rest impossible to see at a distance. Emily slid a hand along to cold, granite wall. It was just as it had been in her dream. Instead of panic, she felt like she was outside herself, watching the scene play out from far away.

She would likely run screaming for the hole and try to claw her way up and out if she *didn't* displace herself that way. The eerie déjà vu reminded her of old "Twilight Zone" episodes she used to watch with her mom on TV late on Saturday nights.

Mom. Emily wondered what she must be thinking by now. Knowing her, she probably had all of the police department's First Precinct (and maybe a few others) out looking for the girls. Her dad was probably pacing the floor and trying to retrace her steps for the day. She hoped at least one of them would think to look at the sinkhole in the neighborhood and see the bikes beside the tree. The twisting in her stomach was replaced with a lump that felt like it weighed twenty pounds.

She and Sarah walked on, not speaking, for at least the length of five city blocks. Fortunately, the path was straight and they knew how to get back to their starting point if they discovered only a dead end.

The strange mix of smells grew stronger and they heard a faint metallic clanking up ahead. Emily figured they must be getting close to some kind of sewer vent or old steam pipe judging from the sound. The tunnel, which had been gradual decline for the majority of their journey, leveled out for a few hundred feet or so before switching slope and becoming a steep incline. The girls took long strides and deep breaths, hoping that some kind of relief was at the top of the long, dark hill beneath the city.

Emily could see the top of their climb just ahead in the beam of her flashlight. The tunnel appeared to level off again and the bend blocked her view once more. Instead of feeling hopeful, her unease boiled up, making the hairs on her neck stand on end. As they neared the crest, the basement smell wafted down the corridor in a gust.

"What the?" Emily said as she reached the top.

"Oh, *great.*"

The girls were standing at a crossroads of sorts. The tunnel they had been in for more than a half hour met three others in some kind of large, round room. One of the openings at the convergence was covered by a thick, wooden door on rusty hinges as large as Emily's wrist. Looking up, she noticed the ceiling was much higher here. It was also covered with a network of ancient looking boards. A few looked like they had graffiti on them, but when she looked at the lowest planks up close with the flashlight, the words were so faded she couldn't make out what they said.

"Man. My mom was just saying something about old tunnels under the city. She said she saw one not too long ago. I wish I'd been paying more attention, I can't remember what they were for," Emily said.

"Which way do you think we should go?" Sarah asked.

"I guess we should try the door—it looks pretty official." Emily turned the cold metal latch and tried to pull it open. It would move a bit, but there was clearly a lock or something preventing it from opening on the other side.

"That'll not budge," said a deep, graveled voiced from the shadows at their left. The girls shrieked and jumped together in fear. "No need for that, now. I mean ya' no harm. Lost, are ya'?"

Emily and Sarah remained silent and still. Emily's hand was trembling so badly that she couldn't raise the flashlight in the direction of the voice. She was sure some part of her was trying to prevent her from seeing what was there. Images from her dreams flooded back into her mind and suddenly felt faint. Her knees gave a weak bounce and Sarah grabbed her around her torso in a strained attempt to keep Emily standing. "Whoa, now!" the voice called.

Emily could tell her feet were no longer on the floor, but her brain could not make any sense of what the rest of her body was telling it. The thing stepped out of a dark tunnel and swept her up before Sarah could let her tumble to the floor. He sat her down on the stone like she was some sort of small, breakable doll.

Emily looked at Sarah and saw an expression she'd never seen on anyone before—terror. Her eyes were stretched wide open and her lips were pulled into a strange, open curve. She slowly raised a hand to point at him, but words failed to leave her mouth. Turning her head to face the thing, Emily understood Sarah's reaction.

The last thing she remembered was looking at the boar man from her dream.

CHAPTER 10

When Emily opened her eyes, everything around her had a warm glow. She struggled for a few moments to remember where she was, and when the memory came back to her, she bolted upright. A wave of dizziness and nausea hit her that she could barely contain. After fighting off another black-out, Emily looked around and saw Sarah sitting near her feet. The boar man adjusted the mantle in a lantern and placed it on the floor near the old wooden door.

"Argh, I hate it when that happens," he complained. "Am I really *that* bad? Honestly?"

Emily hesitated. "Uh..."

"Just come out and say it already! 'You're the most hideous thing I've ever seen.' Come on, I can take it."

"I just... haven't ever seen anyone who looks like you before. I mean, you know, with a," Emily stalled, "hairy face and all." She hoped that would satisfy him long enough that she and Sarah could make a break for it—as soon as the feeling came back in her legs. Emily felt the nagging need to tell him the truth about why she fainted push aside her desire to flee. "Actually, I had a dream about someone like you. That's why I just... flaked out."

His eyes narrowed and he leaned over Emily, his breath hitting her in the forehead. She cringed, fearing he might lash out, or worse. Her eyes darted up at him and she saw that the hairs that covered his skin were a deep auburn. The long teeth that curved up from his jaw were not nearly as long as those of the creature that had startled her so badly in her nightmare, but this one was only a foot away, making it much more terrifying. She waited, trembling, for something awful to happen. Instead, Emily heard the boar man sniffing her.

A loud, boisterous laugh filled the round room. Emily and Sarah shot looks of surprise at each other and then up at the creature holding his belly and clearly getting a joke that they didn't. "You're a Seer! I bet your ancestors come from where? Ireland? Scotland?"

Emily was confused, but answered, "Scotland and Wales, I think."

"Well, *that* explains it. Ya' have a lot of 'feelings' about things, too, I reckon. Probably know when someone is up to no good, right?" Her bewildered look and shift in body language must have answered for her because he continued, "One of the Seers and didn't even know it. Hmph! Ya' saw a little bit of the Underground in a dream and had no idea what was going on!" His laugh boomed again and echoed down the tunnels.

"Hey, why is that so funny?" Emily shouted. She didn't like being the butt of jokes, and she certainly wasn't about to let someone (or some*thing*) she just met make her feel like a fool. Her cheeks flushed with rage. Using a reserve of courage she didn't even know she had, she stood up and put her hands on her hips, but the top of her head barely reached the boar man's chest. He stifled his amusement and barely held in a chuckle with a hairy, three-fingered hand over his mouth. Emily's eyes narrowed. "Can you *please* tell us exactly what is happening?"

"Okay, okay. First off, name's Lolfus. I was just heading home when I heard the two of ya' in the roundhouse here, so I thought I'd come have a look. How'd ya' get down here, anyway?"

This time, it was embarrassment that flushed Emily's cheeks. "We, uh, fell into a sinkhole."

"Arrrgh! I told em' they were doing nothing but stirring up trouble," Lolfus grumbled and shifted his eyes to the floor. His feet kicked at invisible rocks and he swayed nervously.

"Who?" Sarah spoke up.

"Malrich and his pals. I shouldn't be saying anything to ya' about *any* of this, but I reckon you got some right to know seeing as how you're here because of their doings," he said. "Ya' probably figured out by now that those sinkholes were no accident." Emily and Sarah locked eyes for a moment and looked back at Lolfus, eager for more information.

"If they weren't an accident, then what happened?" Emily asked.

Lolfus bent down and lifted the lantern, avoiding Emily's face, and tried to change the subject, "Why don't we get walking, heh? This is no trouble to be concerned with, just old spats getting stirred up again. Come on then, I suppose you want to get out of here." He waved his hand for them to follow him into the tunnel to the left of the old door. Emily and Sarah didn't argue, instead they brushed themselves off and followed their host.

Sarah had picked up Emily's flashlight sometime during her fainting episode and was using it to investigate the walls and ceiling around them. This section of tunnel was made up of brown, rounded stones packed closely together instead of the massive stretches of granite they had seen in the other. Not far into the corridor, the air became thick and damp. Emily thought she caught a bit of mold and fish odors in the air and assumed they must be fairly close to the river. "Mr. Lolfus? Where are we exactly? You know, in relation to what's up *there*," Emily pointed at the ceiling as he peered over his shoulder to make eye contact. The gesture gave Emily an odd feeling of comfort.

"No mister, just Lolfus. I suppose right here... we're under the old Customs Building on Main. I don't think that's what it is anymore, but I can't recall. These things change so often, ya' know, and I don't exactly get out much," he drifted off into thought for several steps. "We're heading for the river, in case you're curious. There's an out for ya' near the old mill on the canal, and the only safe one, too."

The three came to an intersection at the end of their corridor and turned right. About the length of a city block up ahead, Emily could see the tunnel in which they were walking opened into a huge room bustling with sounds and movement. When she was closer, she realized it was the bizarre marketplace she had seen in her dream last night, only this time it was filled with activity. Sarah, unlike Emily, was not at all amazed by the sight. She grabbed Emily's hand with her own trembling, sweaty one. Emily gave her a slight squeeze of reassurance and heard Sarah take a deep breath.

"Hey, Lolfus? What have you got there?" asked a voice up ahead.

"Oh, uh, some lost kids. Fell in a sinkhole. I'm just taking them to the mill."

"You know you can't do that," the voice replied. The tone made Emily's skin crawl. "Malrich needs to know about this—they could be *spies*."

"Ha!" Lolfus bellowed. "Who sends children to spy? Really, Günter, ya've been in these stones for far too long."

"That may be so, but I know trouble when I see it," the voice sounded closer, but Emily could not locate its source. Sarah tugged her hand and she laid eyes on what Sarah had been staring at, her jaw hanging in disbelief: the face and shoulders of a small, pale man, jutting right out of the wall. Emily looked closer to see if he had just squeezed through some kind of tight opening, but realized then that he was moving along beside them as they walked. He peered at them through squinted eyes, his top lip curling back. Sarah let out a tiny whimper.

"Don't mind him," Lolfus said over his shoulder. "These gnomes all act like they work here, but really they just moan and complain." He didn't look anything like any gnome Emily had read about or seen a statue of in any of the neighborhood gardens.

"We do *not*!" Günter said, stepping fully out of the wall and in front of Lolfus. The gnome was smaller than Emily and barely reached the old rope belt holding up the boar man's pants. His skin was smooth and so pale that it seemed to glow with its own light. The only thing that looked remotely typical of a gnome was his long, pointed beard.

He was clearly angry and began shouting at Lolfus in a language neither girl understood, but Emily thought most of it sounded like he was trying to clear his throat. Their guide leaned down and began trying to shush the outburst, looking around the room nervously. A few nearby peddlers looked in their direction and began whispering with each other and sneaking glances at Emily and Sarah. The activity in the market seemed to fade out and all grew quiet, except, of course, for the angry gnome whose pale complexion was turning a sickly shade of blue.

There had been only a few times in her life that Emily wished she could either shrink to the size of an ant or become totally invisible—and this was one of them. Every head in the cavernous room turned and looked in their direction. Lolfus finally resorted to grabbing up Günter and putting his huge hand across the gnome's face to quiet him. The tiny man clearly had more strength than his size led Emily to believe. He kicked at Lolfus and pounded his hairy arm with his fists. "Ouch! Ya' bugger! That's no way to treat a friend," Lolfus cried and dropped Günter to the floor. He ran back into the stone wall like some kind of ghost, his maniacal laugh echoing into the distance. "Should

have known—he bit me. Can't trust one of them."
He winced and shook his hand. Emily could see a
vicious wound on one of his fingers that looked
like it had been made by a shark. The hand looked
like one from a Dr. Seuss book, only with strange
hoof-like nails and wiry reddish hairs instead of
pristine white gloves.

"I thought gnomes were supposed to be all cute
and helpful," Sarah said. Lolfus froze, locked eyes
with her, and let loose another resounding laugh.
The girls couldn't help but laugh with him; it was
the most contagious sound they had ever heard.

CHAPTER 11

Lolfus led the girls through tables and booths covered with shoes, coats, pots and pans, and even what looked like miniature canon balls. Emily was fascinated by the marketplace. Her eyes took in every detail she could capture in the strange place. The boar-like people were all different colors, some were dark like the one from her dream, a few were auburn like Lolfus, and even more were pink with white hairs, just like the pigs from the storybooks Emily read as a child. She guessed that the ones without long lower teeth, or tusks, must be the females, though their style of dress was nearly identical to the males. Everyone wore long, loose pants with sweaters or tunics. Most had weatherproof overcoats or jackets over their wide shoulders and old, worn work boots on their feet.

"What's that ya' have there, Lolfus?" asked a pink female from behind a table of rusty old lanterns, most with cracked or filthy glass surrounding the mantles.

He met her eyes for only a second before turning his gaze to the floor in front of him. "Oh, uh, these two? Lost. Just taking them to the ladder at the mill."

"Very kind of ya'," she smiled. Emily wasn't certain because of the low light, but she was pretty sure the pink lady's cheeks flushed red. Before she could add another flirtatious comment, a roaring voice bellowed across the enormous room.

"Loooolfuuuus!" Their guide's spine straightened and he wiped at his coat, failing to either smooth out the wrinkles or remove the dirt. Two large boar men rounded the corner at the end of the market aisle and strode towards Emily, Sarah, and Lolfus. The two girls instinctively stepped behind him. "Lolfus! I have a good mind to send you out to the coal shafts! Günter tells me you have topsiders. Is that so?" the man growled.

"That's right. I was taking them to the mill. They're just children, not part of this."

"You can *never* tell with that cunning lot! It is probably some kind of trick. You've seen yourself what that evil Tucker has tried already." Emily had a sinking suspicion that the "Tucker" he mentioned was Mayor Tucker. She and Sarah exchanged worried looks behind Lolfus's back. "Where are they?" he shouted. The pink lady in the booth beside them took a step back.

"Malrich, I tell ya' they don't even know what's going on, just fell into one of the holes."

"A fall like that and not even a scratch, am I right?" Malrich asked.

Emily took a deep breath and stepped out from behind Lolfus, "Actually, we sort of slid down, not fell."

Malrich jerked his head back as though someone had just thrown something in his direction. "What's this? It dares to speak for itself? I told you this was no accident, these are Tucker's agents!"

"Sir, I'm not sure who Tucker is, but I promise we're not here to cause trouble. We really are just trying to get home. Our parents probably have the police and half of our neighborhood out looking for us." Malrich stepped forward and leaned over to get a look at Emily face to face. She fought hard the urge to flinch when he snorted hot breath across her cheeks. The wiry black hairs on his brow nearly touched her forehead. Emily had had many stare-offs with Max in the past and was confident she could stand her ground as long as necessary, unless, of course, Malrich decided to lash out at her with one of his massive hands. She made fists, digging her nails into her palms, and counted to ten. He stood upright and looked down his flattened nose at her.

"That may be true, little one, but you cannot leave, not now."

"Malrich," Lolfus interrupted, but was cut off with a sharp look from he dark, menacing boar man behind Malrich.

"No, they stay until the topside matter is settled. I'll consider them our insurance that things resolve smoothly and quickly." Malrich turned to his companion and said, "Alochar, have a gnome sent to Tucker and his pets to let them know about our recent... acquisition." He nodded and walked quickly back the way he came.

Lolfus groaned and shook his head with displeasure. "Ya' can't really think this is a good idea? They'll just retaliate, fake some sort of gas line accident again," he said.

"Oh, I think it's the best idea I've had in a long time. For now, you're in charge of our guests here. I have eyes all over these tunnels, and you'd be wise to remember that if you consider trying to escort them out." Malrich paused to make sure Lolfus understood the seriousness of his statement. "If the topsiders want to strike against us, these two die." With that, he spun on his heel and strode away.

"Did I just hear what I think I heard?" Sarah whispered.

Emily nodded. Her mother's crying face flashed into her mind. Their parents had to be in hysterics by this point, and things didn't look like they were going to improve any time soon. Emily hoped that whatever message the boars were sending to the mayor and the others would motivate them to settle whatever was going on.

"Since we seem to be hostages now," Emily said, "how about letting us know *why*?" Malrich had never said Lolfus should deny them any information. He let out a sigh and motioned them to follow him. Before they moved on, he gave an apologetic smile to the pink lady and a wave of his hand. Though her eyes looked deeply concerned, she forced a grin and nodded her head.

Lolfus led Emily and Sarah to a nook in the wall at the far end of the marketplace. There was a small table and a pair of benches inside that looked as if they may have once been railroad ties. Emily could only guess at their age, which she assumed was many times older than her. The seats had been worn smooth and the table had rounded edge where arms had shaped it for decades. In another nearby nook, she saw three boars playing cards and betting with a variety of things which included a bicycle sprocket, a chrome hubcap, some gaudy costume jewelry, and many more items which Emily did not recognize. They looked up at her and pulled their cards in protectively to their chests.

Sarah sat down in the empty nook and slid over to make room for Emily. Lolfus squeezed himself in across from them, careful not to pin them against the wall with the table. "I suppose I'd better just go straight to the explanation then," he said. Emily and Sarah leaned in, eagerly awaiting details about the latest unfortunate turn in their already unfortunate circumstance. "We Trolls and the topsiders have been at odds since their war began in the 1860s."

"Trolls?" Emily interrupted.

"I know, we don't look exactly like ya' expected, right? Story's always changing. First they say we're covered in warts and eat little children, then all of a sudden we live under bridges—it's all nonsense.

"When the war started, we tried to help as much as we could. Richmond had grown and was really thriving, and it was good for us. We made an agreement with your folk: we'd let them use our place down here to try and save the city from destruction, and in return, they'd make sure we were undisturbed and could go on with our lives no matter which of their armies won. I remember leading spies through the tunnels, that sort of thing. Malrich helped President Davis hide out many times. Nice man, though he never seemed at ease down here. Don't really know why," Lolfus trailed off. Sarah cleared her throat and brought his attention back to the story.

"Every ten or fifteen years since then, some topsider in charge decides that they need a little bit of Troll territory for this or that. We're always having to remind them that the Deal of 1861 is still binding. They don't see us too often, so they tend to forget. Well, the topside council tries to negotiate—that's a fancy word for trying to trick the other side into giving up—and *always* winds up stepping out of line. The first time they started clearing a lot for an office building where one of our main ports is, they found a nice big sinkhole in the mayor's backyard," his eyes twinkled and a hoarse chuckle broke through his lips. "Ya' should have seen how many shades of red he turned when he first saw that pit!" He reveled in that bit of humor for a moment and then looked at Emily and Sarah, "The holes are only a warning, ya' see, just to remind them of who and what they're dealing with when they push too far. Contracts should be respected."

"What's going on now? Why the two holes in two days?" Emily asked.

"Actually, three holes," Lolfus said, averting their eyes. "The gnomes just got though with another one earlier tonight. I hear it's somewhere near Jackson Ward. Probably in one of the triangles where the roads meet, that's the kind of place chosen by tradition—causes an awful lot of trouble topside, but no one gets hurt. We're not out to hurt anyone. Malrich might be in charge, but he doesn't speak for all of us," he insisted. The girls nodded their heads in understanding and he continued. "The topside council is taking it pretty far this time. Ever seen the old power plant right by the canal? We've lived under that stretch of soil since George Washington's men first started to dig that canal, and now the council wants to turn it into some kind of home for topsiders with an underground parking garage. Can you believe it? Taking away the homes of hundreds of Trolls, and no telling how many gnomes, for a *parking garage*?" He shook his head in disgust.

"So the Tucker the mean guy was talking about earlier, is that Mayor Tucker?" Sarah asked.

"It is. He's been the worst of the lot. I think it has something to do with him being a youngster. Uh, no offense meant. Tucker has been trying to test the limits with the Underground since he took office last year, and I fear it is only going to get worse. Malrich and his lot will not tolerate his disrespect for our agreement, even if it was made almost one hundred and fifty years ago. That's hardly a blink of an eye for us."

"Exactly how long have you all been down here?" Emily asked.

"I think it was 1730 we moved in. We worked on the tunnels for years before that, of course. When the English got wise and started brining

German craftsmen over to help with the city's planning and building, we came along, too. That's the custom. They'd always treated us well, so we went where they went." Lolfus hung his head and fell quiet in reflection. Emily could tell the way things had changed since those years was a burden on him and wondered if all of the other creatures here shared the same feeling. An aching heaviness grew in her chest.

Lolfus reminisced about old times for a while, and then he left the table to trade an old brass belt buckle for a few boiled potatoes and gave them to Emily and Sarah. The girls had never been so grateful for plain potatoes before, as both had secretly feared they may have to eat something disgusting like muskrats—or worse.

After their meal, he led them through several short and winding tunnels lined with doors made of old pallet wood, scrap sheet metal, and even old road signs. Emily heard all sorts of sounds coming from behind those doors, from slightly out of tune accordion music to arguments and laughter. Smells of cooking, exotic spices, and lamp oil wafted throughout the corridors. With the exception of the damp stone walls, it reminded her of the big apartment building her uncle had lived in near the college downtown.

They reached a tunnel that was both wider and higher than the rest. At the end was a door at least eight feet tall. It was a *real* door, Emily noticed, not one cobbled together with found materials like the rest, and it was easily as thick and as old as the one she and Sarah had found earlier that evening in what Lolfus had called the "roundhouse".

Lolfus pulled a huge brass key from the pocket of his overcoat. He unlocked the door, pushed it open, and stood aside with the lantern aloft to let the girls enter. He hurried around the room lighting lanterns here and there. Emily and Sarah tried to keep their mouths from hanging open in surprise. The more lanterns Lolfus lit, the larger the room appeared, and they could tell already that it was nearly half the size of the marketplace. To the right of the door they had just come through was a long wooden staircase that climbed to a loft shaped like a horseshoe that hugged the walls of the round room. In the shadows, Emily could see bookshelves filled to their bursting point with books old and new. A huge burgundy carpet covered with intricate patterns around its edges rested in the middle of the room. At least a dozen chair-sized cushions were arranged in a circle at the center of the rug around a low table carved with tiny scenes. "Come on, have a seat," Lolfus pointed.

The girls sank into the plump cushions while Lolfus banged around some pots and pans on the far side of the room. "I'll put on a kettle," he said.

"I'm sure ya' two could use some warming up." Emily saw him strike a match and light the burner of a mammoth antique stove. The peculiarity of their situation floated back into her mind and a bit of giggles erupted. Sarah shot her a look mixed with curiosity and fear.

"All this down here, and no one up there has any idea," Emily laughed. She did not really find it all that humorous, but the laughter came in waves because of nerves. Emily imagined this was what happened to people right before they went crazy and did something foolish, like publicly proclaim that their dog was the President of the United States. Much to her surprise, Sarah actually smiled and joined in.

Lolfus joined them in the circle and looked at them from under a wrinkled brow. "Well, that's a change," he said. "And here I was feeling rotten because ya' have to stay here until who knows when."

"Sorry," Emily said. "It's not really funny, we're just nervous, I guess." Sarah nodded in agreement.

"Ah." He looked down at the floor, "I'm really sorry for getting ya' into this. I was hoping to get you to the mill and out before any trouble had time to stir. That bloody gnome, nothing but grief, he is." Lolfus's lip curled as he thought about Gunter and he gave a low snort. "I should get ya' some beds ready," he said. He left the circle and pulled a few blankets out of a large cupboard under the stairs.

"Are all troll homes like this?" Sarah asked.

"Not exactly," he mumbled. The kettle whistled on the stove and called him back to the kitchen. "You two mind pushing some of those cushions together?" has asked as he handed Emily a pile of soft and colorful quilts. They were so large that she was barely able to hold onto them. She figured they must be large enough for Lolfus to have plenty of extra coverage.

While Lolfus prepared tea, Emily and Sarah each arranged two cushions into a bed and selected a blanket. They had fallen heavily into sleep by the time he returned to the circle and placed a tray onto the carved table. He straightened the blankets over the girls' feet and extinguished several of the lanterns. As he climbed the stairs to his own bed in the loft, he growled, "I'll see that ya' get yours soon enough, Malrich."

CHAPTER 12

It was dark. Emily could hear shouting in the distance and the low, guttural sounds of animals. Despite the angry sounds of the voices, she felt compelled to move in their direction. The tunnel she was in was lined with doors like the ones she'd seen on the way to Lolfus's room, only there were many more and branching corridors that looked the same. Lanterns hung every fifty feet or so, illuminating her way. The walls were damp here and a smell of mildew and wet animals clung to the air.

She followed the sounds for what seemed like a great distance, but it was difficult to tell in the muddy timeline of a dream. At the end of the corridor, she found a slick set of granite stairs. The voices where coming from above, so she climbed each step with her hands on those in front of her to keep her balance. There was a rusted metal door at the top that was open halfway. Emily leaned near and heard the snorts and snarls of the Trolls, and their shouts of warning, contracts broken, and consequences.

"A hole every day until these machines are gone from here!" a voice bellowed. She recognized its ferocity—it was Malrich.

"I'm sorry, the Mayor wants you to understand, the plant here is ours. We're just trying to remove another blighted structure from downtown," an eel slick voice replied.

"Blight!" Malrich erupted. "We have over two hundred homes below this *blight*. You have three days to get your wrecking balls off of this land or we deliver the bodies of your missing girls to the front door of your city's newspaper office with notes pinned to their chests explaining every little detail. Now, it's in *your* hands, Benjamin. Tell Tucker to take his little project elsewhere or the war begins. Don't forget—a hole a day. Our helpers might *accidentally* let the next one surprise you topsiders at a place you can't ignore."

Emily heard several sets of heavy footsteps coming towards the door and she looked around for somewhere to hide. As she turned to tiptoe down the stairs, a voice at her back made her freeze in place. "What have we *here*?" Huge hands grabbed her and her feet left the ground. She kicked and writhed to escape, but her captor was too strong.

A rough cloth sack was pulled over Emily's head and everything went black. Deep, echoing laughter rang in her ears like an explosion. There was no escape.

CHAPTER 13

"Hey! Wake up!" Sarah shouted. Emily was flailing her fists at the air and kicking madly. She opened her eyes, looked at her friend, and realized she was safe—for now.

Lolfus came rushing down the stairs, "What is it?" His eyes darted around the room from the door to the girls and then to every shadow. "What's happened?" he asked.

"Just a nightmare," Emily said. "Sorry."

"Right then. Just wanted to make sure if anyone came to tell ya' it was time to go up that, uh, I was ready to go with ya'." Emily noticed that Lolfus seemed a bit startled, but it may have been because he was just awakened by surprise.

He looked strange to her in his pajamas. She thought they were made of some kind of dark blue velvet, but Emily figured it had to be a trick of the light. Still, it was odd to see that his thick neck and enormous shoulders were not layers of clothing beneath his overcoat like she had originally thought—Lolfus was bigger than any professional athlete she had ever seen. The recognition of this made her very uneasy. Malrich and his goons were even larger than Lolfus.

Sarah eventually fell back asleep, but Emily lay on the cushions and stared at the lantern across the room for a long time. It was hard to tell if it was still night or if it had turned into morning since there were no windows to see the sun. She thought of her regular morning routine and felt sick to her stomach she missed her family so much. Mom and Dad had to be going crazy by now, Emily imagined. Before this, she'd never even been a few minutes late coming home from Sarah's house.

Emily had no idea how much time had passed since her nightmare, but eventually, Lolfus lumbered down the stairs in his overcoat and boots. He rubbed his golden eyes and noticed Emily was awake. "You like coffee?" he whispered. She nodded and followed him to the kitchen area.

"Can I talk to you about something?" she asked as he prepared an old percolator and lit the stove. He gave her an affirmative nod and pulled some ornate cups from a nearby cabinet. "Last night, I had another dream. About this place. That mean guy, Malrich, was in it." Lolfus looked at her and she saw his eyes gleaming. Emily continued, "I followed the sounds of an argument up some old stone stairs to a door. He was outside with some others like you, and he was telling a man that there would be a new hole every day until the mayor changed his current plan. He also said that the holes would start showing up in places he wouldn't be able to ignore." She swallowed hard and decided to leave out the part about him killing her and Sarah. "What you said yesterday, about me being some kind of Seer, does that mean what I dream will come true?"

Lolfus thought about it for a moment, turned to face her, and leaned back against a small counter beside the stove. His posture reminded Emily so much of her father that she had to blink back the tears in her eyes. He rubbed his chin and said, "No, I think ya' Seers have more the warning type of dreams. There are things in them that *can* come true, but ya' see it in time enough to change it. Don't worry about what Malrich and his lot are up to. He has enough cunning left in that thick head of his to know better than to have the gnomes sink something important—there would be no more cooperation from the Topside then."

"The *gnomes* are the ones that make the holes?" Emily had assumed that the trolls must have managed it because of their size. Trying to imagine the skinny old man she'd seen come out through the stone wall last night was to blame felt impossible.

"Of course they are. What did ya' think, it was us Trolls?" The confused look on Emily's face must have answered his question. Lolfus rolled his eyes. "It's because of those stupid little statues everyone has now, isn't it? All you topsiders think that gnomes are like garden fairies or something. The truth is, gnomes *can* be helpful, but they only choose to be when they can get something out of it. Most of the time they are just pure malice."

"How did that one last night pass right into the wall?"

"Gnomes aren't quite solid like you and me. They're more like what ya' would call a ghost. Those buggers can pass through soil and stone like ya' and I pass through the air." Lolfus leaned closer to Emily and lowered his voice so she had to strain to understand him, "Careful what ya' say down here, they could be anywhere in these walls listening." She looked around, uneasy with the thought that a hundred or more gnomes could have been watching her sleep.

"I'm going to head down to the market and see what I can find ya' two to eat. All that I have here is some old bread and a few tins of beans," Lolfus said. "Make yourselves at home, but be sure to stay inside my chamber. Going outside of this room without me is not a wise idea, especially after that dream ya' just told me about." He let himself out and Emily heard the distinct click of the lock behind him, a noise that certainly made her feel more like a prisoner than a guest.

Instead of waking Sarah, who looked as though she hadn't slept in weeks, Emily looked around Lolfus's home. His kitchen was clean and tidy. She peeked inside the cupboards and saw dishes arranged just like in any of those on the topside. He had stacks of beautiful plates with glittering silver and gold designs around the pastel flowers that lined their edges. The teacups were dainty and thin. Emily wondered how Lolfus could even hold them in his giant hands.

She moved around the room with a lantern she claimed from a countertop, peering at portraits that decorated the walls in the shadows under the loft. She saw a male troll that looked much larger than Lolfus, but who was the same auburn color. He was dressed in an ornate white shirt with ruffles down the chest. Seated in front of him in the portrait was a female with dark hair and skin who was wearing a long scarlet gown and several jewels. She stared back at Emily with intense golden eyes, much like those of her host.

Emily continued to survey the room and decided to venture upstairs. She came to a row of enormous bookcases that looked like they may have been made from the thick, weather-worn planks of a ship. Holding the lantern close, Emily scanned the shelves and was surprised to see an odd variety of both old and new books. There were ancient looking leather tomes whose names had long faded from their covers, volumes of Victorian medical encyclopedias, science and atomic technology textbooks from the 1950's, even a whole bookcase filled to its bursting point with National Geographic Magazines. She wondered if Lolfus actually read these or if they were part of some strange Troll collection like those she had seen in the market yesterday.

The bookcase at the far end of the row was packed with books about Richmond. Some were so old they were handwritten and decorated. Like the rest of the shelves, it also included many new books about the city. Emily pulled off one that caught her eye as different from the rest—a book of Richmond legends.

She sat down at a desk the size of a small car and placed the lantern on a hook above its surface. Leaning back in the heavy upholstered chair, she began to turn the pages. Almost immediately she found a drawing of a boar man labeled "Troll." The written description on the troll was clearly the product of someone's imagination, but it still wasn't giving her a warm, fuzzy feeling so she decided she'd had enough.

Emily had just closed the book and put it back on the shelf when Lolfus returned with what looked like a small laundry basket of food. Sarah was awakened when he opened the door and her eyes darted around for Emily. "I'm up here," she called to the two below, "I was reading one of your books." She retrieved the lantern from over the desk and went downstairs to inspect Lolfus's finds.

Emily was correct—Lolfus had filled a laundry basket with an odd variety of root vegetables, canned corn, fat loaves of homemade bread wrapped in waxed paper, and even a few Hostess cakes on the side. He pointed to the basket he had placed on the carved table in the center of the room and said, "Hope there's something ya' like in there. I got a little bit of everything I could find." The girls peered in and grabbed handfuls of whatever they thought they could eat quickly, which mostly consisted of bread and chocolate cupcakes. Lolfus went to the kitchen and made another batch of coffee in the percolator. He brought a tray of steaming cups, sugar, and a small can of milk and joined them on a cushion.

Emily had started on a chunk of brown bread, still warm from the oven, while Lolfus was in the kitchen. It was some of the best she'd ever tasted. There was a pleasant chewiness to it, and a flavor she couldn't quite place. "What kind of bread is this?" she asked with her mouth full.

"That's pumpernickel, a good recipe from the old world, too. Gelda just made it this morning,"

Lolfus said. He diverted his eyes and added, "She said to tell ya' hello as well."

"Gelda?" Sarah asked.

"Ya' sort of met her last night. She's the, uh, lady whose table we were at when all the fuss broke out."

"Oh, cool. Is she your girlfriend?" Sarah blurted. Lolfus coughed on his coffee and put his cup gingerly down on the table with his thick hands.

"No, no. Just a nice lady at the market is all. She makes a fine bread."

"Well, if you ask me, it's pretty obvious she likes you, and not in a 'nice lady at the market' kind of way, either," said Sarah. Emily giggled with her mouth full and saw Lolfus getting as nervous and clumsy as a shy schoolboy. "You should ask her out. What do you do around here for dates?"

He cleared his throat, stirred a little more milk into his coffee, and said, "I don't really know, never courted a lady." After a long, awkward stretch of silence he added, "Ya' think she likes me, huh?"

"Even I could see *that*," Emily giggled. Sarah joined in, and even Lolfus couldn't hold in a smile. Their light-hearted breakfast was interrupted by a scrawny gnome sticking his head through the wall beside the door.

"Eh-hem," it said. "Malrich wants to see you Lolfus. Now. These two are to stay here, come alone."

"I'll be right there," Lolfus answered. He leaned towards Emily and said, "Remember what I told ya' this morning? Make sure to get her up to speed, okay?" Emily nodded.

Lolfus had a look of concern as he closed the door and locked it behind him once again. Emily could tell that something was off, something was not going as planned. She didn't have a good feeling about it at all.

CHAPTER 14

Emily and Sarah finished off all of the bread and sugary treats their stomachs could hold and cleaned up the mess as well as they could. Sarah asked, "So, what is it that's so secret, something I need to know?"

Emily motioned for her to join her back at the center of the room on the cushions—she wanted to be as far away from the walls as possible. "You know that creepy gnome we saw last night?" Sarah nodded. "Well, there are a *ton* of them down here and they can all pass through the stone walls and whatever like it's nothing but air. Lolfus said for us to be careful what we talk about because they could be listening at any time."

"That stinks!" Sarah paused for a moment and narrowed her eyes. "We should test them. You know, talk about something ridiculous like it's the truth and see how fast they tattle. If anyone comes back to us, we'll just say we were joking and they took in the wrong way," she whispered.

"I don't know. What if they can't take a joke? Or worse, what if they act on a misunderstanding before they question us about anything? It could be *really* bad."

"I don't think it could be any worse than sitting around this cave waiting for something to happen." Emily shrugged and gave a hesitant nod. Sarah had a way of making crazy ideas seem like the sanest option.

A rattle and clank at the door startled them back to the present. Lolfus came in wearing a heavy scowl. "Uh, everything okay?" Emily asked.

"Fine, fine. Just been reminded by Malrich that I'm to keep a close eye on ya' and not get any funny ideas about sneaking ya' out of here. That rot even threatened to send me off to the coal shafts with the Kobold if I didn't mind my path." The girls' looks of confusion and concern must have asked the question on their minds before their mouths could voice it. "Kobold? They're only the worst kind of gnome there is. Well, they *used* to be gnomes. They're the ones who did too much mining back in the old country and sort of lost their wits. It'll happen. Awful wicked things, too. I can't believe you never heard the stories about some of the Kobold who butchered topside lords and kings." Now Sarah and Emily were officially worried. The gnomes were bad enough, but talk of some that were even more nasty and inhospitable than the one they'd met the night before did not sit well.

"Anyway, ya' don't have anything to worry about. I suspect that things are about to be worked out. Malrich mentioned that he had the gnomes finish another sinkhole last night that he thinks will push Tucker back to his senses in a day or two."

"Another hole? Where?" Sarah asked.

Lolfus looked down at the floor and kicked at some imaginary something near his feet. "The Belleview Elementary School."

"No way!" Emily shouted. "That's where most of our friends go. Did anyone get hurt?"

"No, just pulled down the whole playground is all. It's the biggest sinkhole so far." In a low tone, almost a growl, he added, "Malrich was laughing about it. He's real amused with himself this time."

"And you really think *this* is going to make the mayor change his mind about the old power plant?" Emily asked.

"Why wouldn't it? No mayor in the past has ever held on to their plans against us Trolls after a threat on children. They know better."

"I'm not so sure this one does," Sarah added. "He knows we're down here and hasn't done anything about it yet."

"Hmph," Lolfus muttered as he gave Sarah's comment some thought. Rubbing his bristled chin, he said, "True. I think it's the numbers that will sway him this time around, though. I hate to say it, but maybe he thinks two children are expendable. No way he'd let anything happen to hundreds." Emily wanted to believe Lolfus was right about Tucker, but something in the bottom of her stomach didn't feel quite right, and she was certain the pumpernickel was not to blame. A loud knock at the door cut through their thoughts and made them all jump.

"Ah, must be Heinrich," Lolfus grunted as he approached the door. "I was waiting for him." He opened the door a crack to confirm his suspicion, and then swung it wide with a gesture for the guest to enter.

A huge pale Troll entered and gave the girls a curious glance. His pink skin was almost white under the cream-colored hairs that covered his face and hands. He was dressed in many layers of light gray clothing that, when combined with his complexion, gave him a ghostly appearance. "Hallo," he said in a whisper. Emily and Sarah returned his greeting with small smiles and insecure waves.

"Girls, this is Heinrich. He's Gelda's brother." It was then Emily realized why he looked so familiar—the two could have been twins. Lolfus gave Emily and Sarah a look behind Heinrich's back that told them to keep quiet about that morning's conversation concerning his sister.

The Trolls joined the girls at the ring of cushions. "Can I get ya' something?" Lolfus asked Heinrich.

"No, no. You are too generous. I'm here in service." Emily and Sarah exchanged looks of confusion. "I just heard about the school."

"Then ya' understand why we need to be ready. If Tucker drags his heels, we'll have no time to spare." Lolfus motioned them all to lean in towards the carved table at the center of the circle. Barely audible, he said, "I have a plan." Heinrich raised his brow in interest and the girls were more confused than ever.

"For what?" Emily asked.

"To get ya' out of here and to put a stop to Malrich's tyranny for good. We'll need your help, of course."

"Ours?" Sarah squeaked. The idea of opposing Malrich didn't sound like an easy one to Emily, either, but her instincts were telling her it was the right thing to do if she wanted to stay alive.

"We're in," Emily said. Heinrich blinked in amazement while Lolfus gave her a confident grin and a pat on the back that nearly knocked her to the floor.

"All right then, here's what we need to do..."

CHAPTER 15

Lolfus gave them very detailed instructions about their roles in his strategy to get the girls out of the troll underground. Emily was a little distressed when she learned that his "plan" basically involved someone creating a distraction while the girls made a run for it and hoped to avoid trolls and gnomes on their way out. After the past two days, she was much more open to things she would not have done under normal circumstances. Things had stopped being normal for her the day the first sinkhole appeared in her neighborhood.

In the loft of his quarters, Emily watched as Lolfus emptied a wooden crate filled with books. Her furrowed brow must have been giving away all of her jumbled thoughts, because Lolfus said, "Don't ya' worry. There are lots of good folks down here who are just as tired of Malrich's attitude as I am. Believe me, this is not a new problem." Emily had figured that the trouble with Malrich ran much deeper than his conflict with Mayor Tucker, but she wasn't sure exactly how bad things were. If there were enough Trolls ready to help Lolfus with his mission, why didn't they just kick Malrich out or something? What exactly were they so afraid of? "Besides, this plan is pretty much our only chance right now," he added.

Sarah joined them upstairs and tossed Emily an apple and another Hostess cupcake. She took one look at Lolfus's box and said, "Oh, wait just a minute! You're not planning on putting *us* in that, are you?"

"Only if you can't keep it down," Emily said, cutting a sideways glance at Lolfus. He tried to hide a smile, but couldn't manage it. Sarah finally caught on to the joke and gave a huge, dramatic sigh and rolled her eyes so far that Emily thought for a moment that they may turn loose from her skull.

"We should know something by tonight," Lolfus said. "Heinrich will hear from Malrich about Tucker's reaction by dinnertime at the latest. That's when he'll have Heinrich give the gnomes the order for another sinkhole if he needs."

"Heinrich works with the gnomes?" Sarah asked.

"He follows orders, and if following orders means working with the gnomes, that's what he does. He's a General, takes commands only from Malrich." Lolfus must have read the looks on the girls' faces because he added, "Yes, I'm certain I can trust him. Our families have ties that go back more than a thousand years. Heinrich will be on the side of right." He shelved the last few books from the crate, closed it with a thud, and sat down in the enormous chair beside the desk. With a sigh, Lolfus said, "Now, we wait."

The hours between lunch and dinner dragged on without mercy. Emily and Sarah taught Lolfus how to play Crazy Eights with a tattered deck of cards he found in a kitchen cupboard. He told them stories about how the city looked before the skyscrapers were built, when deer would still come down to the riverbank to drink. They talked about books and discovered that Lolfus was quite fond of the Harry Potter series, "A tale of magic like those of old!" he cheered. Eventually, the conversation came around to the topic of Gelda.

"What would it take for you to get to know her better?" Sarah asked. Emily knew Sarah's brain was always cooking up a scheme, and it worked especially hard when matchmaking was involved. She had once tried to set up a love connection between Emily and a neighbor her age from the next block, Sean. Sarah failed to notice that Sean's only hobby involved falling off of his skateboard and crashing into things like street signs and parked cars—without wearing a helmet. Emily put an abrupt end to her friend trying to play Cupid with her after that incident.

Lolfus picked up the cards from the table and began to shuffle them, dropping several more with each failed attempt. It was obviously a difficult task to manage when you only had two thick fingers and a thumb that looked like it barely bent. "I wouldn't even know where to begin," he said. "We've known each other since we were children. Our families were close, but we never pursued anything...romantic."

"Why don't you just get Heinrich to tell her you'd like to take her to dinner or something?" Sarah asked. Emily had to admit, it sounded like a reasonable idea.

Malrich shifted his weight and handed the deck of cards to Emily to deal. "Well, I'll give that some thought. It's not the usual way we do things here, but I guess I have nothing to lose but a little pride if she says no."

They played three rounds of cards and were about to begin a fourth when the knock they were waiting for sounded from the door. Malrich hurried to answer it and exchanged a few hushed words with the person on the other side. After the brief conversation, he closed the door and turned to them, "Okay, time for me to run a quick errand. Looks like I'll have to go and, uh, trade for some new books after all."

"So, Tucker's *still* not cooperating?" Sarah whispered, looking around at the stone walls warily. The possibility of eavesdropping gnomes was making both of the girls especially paranoid.

"Apparently not. I don't think he has any idea how serious this could get," Lolfus said. Emily was both worried and relieved that he didn't feel the need to elaborate on just how bad his idea of "serious" might be, especially after what happened at Belleview Elementary. "While I'm gone, Malrich will have Heinrich come to stand guard over ya'." He leaned in very close and whispered, "That's when you run. Follow the turns I told ya', stick together, and don't stray off course. Things will be fine."

Emily and Sarah exchanged worried looks. There was something off in the tone of his voice that made the uncertainty of their situation even more uncomfortable than it already was.

Lolfus stomped up the stairs and made a huge clamor when he loaded an armful of mixed items in the crate to exchange at the bookstore. He came back down with the box just as a loud knock erupted from the door. "Hold on, ya'," Lolfus shouted. He sat the crate on the floor and unlocked the door to find Alochar standing on the other side. "What do ya' want? Where's Heinrich?"

"Malrich sent me to keep an eye on the spies while you go topside. Heinrich's busy," he said.

Emily knew right away that things could go very wrong with their plan now. As long as Heinrich was on guard duty, he'd make sure the corridors were clear and tell them when to run. With Malrich's head henchman there instead, they were stuck.

Lolfus stepped aside and let Alochar enter, giving Emily and Sarah a serious look and a nod when the other boar-man's back was to him. "Well, then. I'll only be a short while; Kelly will be waiting for me at the basement door when I get there. Don't ya' worry, we'll be back at those cards before you know it." He looked determined as he hoisted the crate, stepped through the enormous door, and then poked his head back inside, "Oh, Alochar, the young one there can make a fine cup of coffee. You should give it a try." Lolfus gave Emily a look like there was something she should already know about that comment, but she couldn't figure it out for the life of her. Still, something was making the hairs on her neck stand on end—a sure sign that things were either very right or very wrong.

Alochar gave a grunt in reply and then sat down in the seat Lolfus had occupied just a few minutes earlier, but the mood in the room was far less pleasant. Emily and Sarah mostly looked at their own feet, pulled imaginary lint off of their clothes, or found any other distraction to avoid the eyes of Malrich's henchman. When Emily did take the chance to sneak a quick look in his direction, she found that he was glaring at them both. "Umm... Anyone want to play cards?" she asked, obviously trying to break the tension.

Emily looked at Sarah, who gave a nervous shrug, and then to Alochar. He said nothing, but continued to glare, so Emily tried a different approach. "Lolfus was no good. I beat him at nearly every game. Think you could do better?"

Alochar puffed his chest out at the challenge. "Hmph. I could triumph over Lolfus in any sport or test of skill."

"Okay, then," Emily said. "Let's see what you've got. Do you know how to play poker?"

In a voice that was almost a growl, he replied, "Just deal."

After they had played three hands, Emily offered Alochar coffee. "You and Sarah can make this round a one-on-one and I'll watch the stove. You're winning two out of three anyway, so I don't figure I have much chance at saving the game." Emily was determined to figure out what was so special about her coffee. She never really thought of it as good, but her parents often drank it without voicing any complaints, so maybe it was better than she'd given herself credit for.

"Aye, coffee." Apparently Alochar was a troll of few words.

Sarah looked at Emily as she stood and her eyes asked a thousand questions. Emily had no answers to give, so she shrugged and headed for the kitchen. A percolator was sitting on the stovetop, so she filled it with water and dropped in the little metal cup to receive the coffee grounds. She had to grope around in the dim light to find the right cupboard, but she located the coffee can and noticed a small brown bottle nestled behind it on the shelf. She leaned in and gave it a closer look—it was labeled with an ancient-looking piece of decorative paper that said "Sleeping Daught." It took a moment, but the message Lolfus was trying to send her as he left suddenly became clear. He'd had a backup plan this whole time.

She took a quick look over her shoulder and saw that Alochar and Sarah were deep in concentration, so she grabbed the can of coffee, palmed the tiny bottle, and made her way back to the stove. When the coffee was done, she asked Sarah, "Hey, do you want some, too?" Emily made her eyes wide and plastered a fake smile across her face to send her friend the signal that she should say no and keep playing along. Whatever she was doing seemed to be working.

"Uh... No, I think it will just keep me up too late. Besides, I can't concentrate if I drink coffee," Sarah said.

Emily pulled a cup and saucer from the shelf, quickly poured in the entire contents of the little bottle, and topped it off with coffee. "Milk and sugar, Mr. Alochar?" she asked, careful not to sound too cheery.

"Black."

A light sheen of perspiration formed on Emily's forehead and her hands felt damp and clammy from the sudden burst of nerves. She worried that Alochar might be able to taste the sleep tonic, and she hoped that she had made the coffee strong enough to disguise the flavor. Fighting the tremble of her hands that threatened to give her away, she delivered the cup and saucer to the low table and placed it in front of the troll.

He squinted at the cards in his hand, taking the game far more seriously than Emily had expected, and she hoped that his concentration would work to their advantage. Still contemplating his strategy in the game, Alochar picked up the tiny porcelain cup and drained half of it in one sip. "Mmm. Pretty good," he said.

Emily felt as if a tight band had suddenly been released from her lungs and she could breathe again. So far, so good.

Sarah made her bet with the strange mix of nuts, bolts, washers, and other metal scrap that they were using in place of poker chips and Alochar narrowed his eyes at her. With a growl, he pushed a heap of metal into the pile at the center of the table and then grabbed his coffee, emptying the cup with a defiant toss of his head. "Let's see what you've got, topsider," he said.

Sarah laid her cards out on the table—a Flush. Good, but certainly not great. Emily thought that it would probably serve them well if Sarah didn't try *quite* so hard to win. She knew her friend was competitive, but when your opponent in the game might kill you if he loses, it's probably best to let him have the advantage.

Alochar looked smug and Emily was just about to breathe a sigh of relief when she noticed his expression falter. He looked from Sarah to Emily and back again just before his eyes rolled back in his head and he tipped forward, his face slamming into the carved top of the table with a loud, echoing *thud*.

Sarah leaned in to see the cards that he still clutched in his hand. "Aw, man! He had a Royal Flush! I didn't even stand a chance." She sounded almost forlorn.

Again, Emily felt like she had to be the voice of reason in a completely unreasonable situation. "Uh... I just knocked out a troll with a sleeping potion. I think it's time for us to get out of here."

CHAPTER 16

Emily waited, shifting her weight from one foot to another like a horse about to burst out of a starting gate, while Sarah put on her shoes and steeled herself for the half-baked plan they were about to try and execute. After checking her laces at least for or five times, Sarah finally took a deep breath and said, "Well, I guess we'd better go for it." Emily wiped her sweaty palms on her jeans and nodded nervously in agreement.

They walked as quickly and as quietly as they could to the door to the cavernous apartment. The thought that Lolfus had locked them in after giving her a clue as to his backup plan didn't hit Emily until her hand grasped the latch. "Oh, please be open..." With a *click*, the latch released and she slowly pulled the door open far enough to peek out into the corridor to check for guards. Seeing no one, she turned back to Sarah and held up her crossed fingers for luck and watched as her friend returned the sign.

They held hands tightly and stepped out into the long hallway. All they had to do now was move as fast as they could and remember the directions Lolfus had given them to the ladder and the hatch that opened onto a city sidewalk near the train station. Emily didn't think it would be too difficult, but she found it harder than she had expected because it was impossible to hear if anyone was coming with her pulse pounding in her ears. She thought Sarah must be having the same problem because they both slowed down at every corner and hesitated much longer than Emily felt they should have.

Operating almost entirely on adrenaline, the girls made it to the next-to-last turn in the maze of underground tunnels when they froze at the sound of voices in the corridor ahead. It was too distant to make out what the voices were saying, but Emily could tell that there were at least three of them and those voices were headed towards the girls.

"Oh, crap!" she whispered. "Quick! Back here!" Emily tugged Sarah back a few yards and into a recess in the wall of the corridor at a curve. She hoped that if they stood on their tiptoes, held their breath, and pressed their backs into the wall that the trolls might be so caught up in whatever they were discussing that they would walk right by and not notice. It was dark, and human eyes would definitely have a hard time seeing a figure in that depression in the rock, but Emily had no idea how sensitive the trolls' vision might be—they spent most of their time in the dark, after all.

The voices drew closer and closer, their tones gruff and unfriendly, and Emily thought the trolls would surely hear her heart try and beat its way right out of her chest. She and Sarah held hands so tightly that her fingers were starting to go numb. They flattened themselves against the wall and tried to blend with the stone as well as they could.

Footsteps echoed through the corridor as the group of trolls approached the curve in the passage and the girls' hiding place. Their voices continued, but Emily realized now that they were so close that they were speaking another language. She could only make out a word or two, but she was pretty sure that it was German and she was confident that the topic was not a pleasant one.

Four hulking figures passed by Emily and Sarah without noticing them. After waiting for a few moments to let the trolls travel far enough to round a bend, the girls each took deep breaths and Sarah's lips formed the words, "Oh my gosh," without making a sound.

Emily motioned with her head to move back into the tunnel and continue toward their exit, and Sarah gave a nod in agreement. They drew their courage up and leapt away from the wall, ready to run, when they came face to face with a huge brown mountain of a troll passing through by himself. Rocking back on their heels, both girls let out a squeak of surprise before turning to run the other direction.

A strange sensation overcame Emily, and then she realized that the enormous troll had grabbed her and lifted her just a few inches off of the floor by her shirt and jacket. Her feet were still scrambling, trying to put distance between herself and the rumbling growl that had erupted behind her. From the corner of her eye she saw that Sarah was caught in the same position.

"Well, what have we here?" the troll said. His voice seemed thick and grim with amusement, and Emily could feel the air rush past her ear as his face moved forward to sniff her. "Oh, methinks Lord Malrich is going to reward me handsomely for this little discovery, yes?" A low, hollow chuckle shook from his chest. "Oh, yes, indeed."

CHAPTER 17

Emily and Sarah sat with their arms tightly hugging their knees against their chests. There was hardly room to move in the tiny cage that they had been crammed into, and every time one of them shifted their weight, the cage swung sickeningly from the bulky chain on which it was suspended.

"Ugh, now we've done it," Sarah whispered. Guards stood at the four corners of the cavernous room, and neither of the girls wanted to draw their attention—not even to ask to use the bathroom.

Emily was afraid to open her eyes for too long. She knew that they had pulled the cage up with the chain and a rusty old pulley that made so much noise she thought sure the people on the streets above them could hear it over the traffic sounds, but she didn't want to know exactly how high up it had gone. Her stomach twisted in knots and she tried her hardest not to throw up in the tight confines she shared with her friend because Sarah would *never* let her forget it. If they lived long enough for it make any difference.

They heard footsteps approaching and barely had time to steady themselves before the enormous wooden door flew open and struck the wall with a thunderous whack. "Well, well..." A seething voice rose up from the floor below them and Emily realized it was familiar in the way it made her skin crawl. She stole a quick glance through her barely-open eyes and saw that it was Malrich.

"I knew that brother of mine couldn't be trusted with this kind of responsibility. It was only a matter of time before you ended up here, spies. Hmph. But it's of no concern to me. In fact, I think your sudden...change of *status* might just help bring the axe down on this foolish power plant business at last." Emily's eyes widened when she saw the evil grin forming on Malrich's face. He looked almost happy, but in an unsettling way, like he was about to crack open their cage and eat them for dinner. She never had the opportunity to ask Lolfus if there was ever any truth in all of those tales about trolls eating people who had crossed them, and now she was regretting it.

"Malrich!" Lolfus boomed as burst into the room. He looked up at the girls through the rusty iron bars and Emily saw a look of deep regret pass across his features before he quickly concealed it. "What's the meaning of this?" he shouted.

"Ah, big brother, you're just in time to say goodbye to your little friends here. They'll be executed in front of Tucker's messenger just before dawn."

"What?" Sarah screamed and Emily felt every muscle in her own body begin to tremble.

"You'll do no such thing! You know as well as I do that killing a topsider goes against everything the Treaty stands for—it will start a war that we're not equipped to fight," Lolfus said, his composure slipping.

Malrich took a few determined steps toward Lolfus, only stopping when their chests collided. Through clenched teeth, Malrich said, "That *human* laughed in the face of the Treaty when he refused to stop his plans of demolishing part of our city to further the interests of his own. As far as I'm concerned, our Treaty has already been nullified. I will do what I need to do in order to protect our kind."

"No, you'll do what you need to do to wield your power over the topsiders. You've always wanted things to turn this way. You've never been satisfied with your authority over our troll city— you want the streets as well," Lolfus pressed.

A menacing laugh escaped Malrich's throat, slowly and softly at first, but it evolved to a frenzied sound in a matter of seconds. "You're more observant than I've given you credit for, brother. Too bad you were not observant enough to keep these vermin from escaping your watch. Guards! Take him."

All four troll guards moved toward Lolfus at once, smoothly drawing swords on their approach. Emily gasped and grabbed at the flat iron bars of the cage as Lolfus attempted to fight off his capture and a blade grazed his arm, slicing through the thick overcoat and the layers of fabric he wore below it. A dark stain surrounded the gash while the guards pinned him to the floor and pressed the side of his face to the cold stone. "No need to make this any harder, Majesty," one of them said.

Majesty? Sarah and Emily exchanged confused looks as another guard wrapped a heavy chain around their friend's arms and fitted him with some sort of metal belt at his waist, firmly binding the two together with a padlock the size of Emily's hand.

"No! It's not his fault! He didn't know what we were planning," Emily pleaded.

The guards dragged Lolfus to his feet and led him out the door with Malrich at their heels. He turned to give them another wicked smile over his shoulder, "Too little, too late, topsider."

CHAPTER 18

The only sound in the chamber after Malrich and his henchmen led Lolfus out was the sound of Sarah and Emily's panicked breathing. They were both trembling, not from cold, but from nervous shock. "What are we going to do now?" Emily whispered.

"No idea. I was kind of hoping that Lolfus had come to rescue us, but it looks like that didn't go quite the way I'd wanted," Sarah said.

"Seriously, don't kid around. They might do the same thing to him that they are talking about doing to us and it's *our* fault."

"Oh. Yeah. Now that you put it like that, I guess we are sort of responsible, aren't we?"

"If we had just stayed away from that sinkhole, none of this would be happening now—we'd be back at home with our families and Lolfus would be safe, too," Emily said. Tears stung her eyes and she fought to hold them back. She had somehow held it together this long, and she was certainly going to try and stay strong until she just couldn't stand it anymore and all of the regret, sadness, and homesickness came pouring out of her. Sadly, she felt like her breaking point was growing closer and closer by the minute.

"We can still try to figure out a way to escape or to get Malrich to change his mind or *something*," Sarah said. She looked thoughtful as she rubbed her chin and tried to think of a solution. "Remember that time when we accidentally destroyed your brother's entry for the big robotics competition when we tried to get the robot to chop boards in half like a karate master?" Emily nodded, the memory bringing a bit of a smile to the edges of her lips. "We never thought we'd get out of that one, but we did. We fixed it. I bet there's some way we can fix this, too, but only if we hurry."

"You might be right," Emily said.

"Of course I'm right! I'm always right. Besides, this cage is totally gross and uncomfortable and I don't plan on staying in it for any longer than I have to." Sarah started fidgeting in a desperate attempt to reach the pockets of her jeans. The sudden movements caused her weight to shift and the cage began to swing, pushing Emily's fear of heights to its limits. She squeezed her eyes closed out of reflex.

"Can you *please* not do that!" Emily snapped.

"Sorry, but it was totally worth it—see?" Sarah said. Emily opened her eyes just enough to see Sarah's outstretched palm holding an assortment of weird metal trinkets. "I won these from that mean guy Alochar during the poker game. Think we could pick that lock?"

Emily shrugged. Neither she nor Sarah had ever successfully picked a lock before, but they had never been in a situation where their lives depended on it, either. "I sure hope so."

Sarah selected a small rod that was flattened and slightly bent at one end, like part of a screwdriver with a damaged tip, and handed the rest of the trinkets to Emily. "Here, hold these. I'm going to try this one first." She reached through the bars of the cage and had to press her cheek up against them to reach the lock that held their tiny prison closed. Her hands worked the lock in all directions, the makeshift lock-picking tool scraping and clicking the old metal all the while. Suddenly, she froze and said, "Hey, I think I might have it!" A look of pure concentration settled on her face, but it was soon displaced by a look of panic and a *clink* of metal hitting the stone floor.

"You dropped it?" Emily asked with a sigh. Sarah looked completely defeated when she nodded in response. The rod that Sarah had selected was their best option from the little group of her poker winnings. Emily saw something else among them that seemed like it was worth trying, though—a long, dark, flattened iron nail that had probably been made at some blacksmith's anvil more than a hundred years earlier. "Here, see if you can do anything with this one," she said, "And try hard not to drop it this time."

Sarah rolled her eyes, but Emily could tell that she felt relieved at the second chance. Emily chewed her bottom lip as Sarah worked at the lock again. The cage felt tighter and tighter as the moments passed and soon Emily was sweating and wishing she could take off her jacket, but there wasn't enough room for her to move her arms the way she'd need to in order to wiggle out of it.

Sarah's brow furrowed, her arms strained to reach the lock, when—*clunk*—her eyes grew wide. "It opened!" It took a minute or so for her to wiggle the lock up and out of the loop on the cage door, but eventually it fell to the floor with a horrible clatter.

"Shh! We're going to have every one of those guards back in here in a second," Emily hissed.

"It's not like I meant to do it," Sarah said. "Okay, I got the lock open, now you figure out how to get us down from here. It's too far to jump without getting hurt, and I don't think either one of us could carry the other through those tunnels and up a ladder, so that's out."

Emily looked up and saw that the chain that held the cage only rose a few feet to the pulley on the ceiling. From there the chain wrapped over the pulley, stretched downward at an angle, and was secured to a massive metal loop attached to the stone floor. She swallowed the lump that had formed in her throat. "Well, we could go up, then down," she said as she pointed to the chain.

"That's brilliant! Who goes first?" Sarah asked.

"Definitely you."

Sarah took a few breaths to compose herself and she reminded Emily a lot of an athlete about to compete. She pushed open the cage door and it swung with a sickening creak. Sarah scooted on her bottom towards the opening and placed one foot on the edge of the cage while letting the other leg hang freely. She squeezed through and twisted her body with one smooth motion while her hands steadied her on the cage's edge.

Emily had a hard time wrapping her mind around how her friend had just gone from sitting with her in a space smaller than a refrigerator to climbing onto the top of the box that had confined her only moments before. She tried to watch Sarah's movements so she could copy them when it was her turn, but every time their weight shifted, the cage rocked and swayed like a boat tossed by rough waves. Emily's knuckles turned white as she gripped the bars and finally looked straight down. It was a bad idea.

"Hey, it's not as hard as it looks," Sarah said as she started her slow journey down the chain and toward the floor with her arms and legs hooked up and over it for support.

"Easy for you to say—you're not paralyzed by a fear of heights."

"Which is worse," she said in a loud whisper, "The fear of heights or the fear of Malrich killing us in an hour or two?"

"Okay, you have a point there," Emily said as she tried to muster up the courage to inch over to the open door of the cage. She slowed her breathing and thought of her parents. She thought of her room. She even thought of her little pest of a brother. All of those things were worth the climb to her, even if her body was having a hard time coming to an agreement with her mind. The last image that flashed through her brain before she finally stuck her feet through the opening was of her parents' faces sick with worry and fear, not knowing where she was or if she was safe. This was her fault and she had to make it right.

Emily kept her eyes pointed in front of her, never looking down. She moved like Sarah had, even though she had only a fraction of Sarah's confidence about what she was doing. It was tough to get a grip on the bars of the cage because her hands were slick with sweat, and the few times her fingers began to slip, she only had to think of home to tighten her hold. Eventually, she made it to the top of the cage despite its wild swinging.

"Take a deep breath, the rest is easy!" Sarah said. From the distance of her voice, Emily assumed that she was already on the floor, but she was too afraid to look and see for herself. "Grab the chain with both hands, swing one leg up and over, then the other, and then cross your ankles and make your way down like an upside-down inchworm."

Emily followed her instructions and managed to get both hands and both legs around the chain, but then she froze and merely clung to the metal for dear life. "Hurry up! I think I hear footsteps in the tunnel!" Sarah called. Emily held her breath and started her descent. She turned all of her focus to the movements of her legs and hands and paid no attention to the amount of distance she had traveled. In less than a minute, she felt Sarah's hands at her back to help steady her. "You're down—just drop!"

"I don't think I can make myself let go," Emily squeaked.

"You'd better figure out a way to make it happen soon because we need to hide. Like, *now*!"

Emily finally peeled herself off of the chain and had to struggle to resist the urge to kiss the cold stone floor. She was trembling, either from fear or from pure adrenaline, but she managed to grab Sarah's hand and make a run for the open door to the corridor. They pressed themselves against the wall beside the doorway and Sarah slowly peeked out and glanced in both directions. "Which way?" she asked.

"I don't know how they brought us in here, so I'll settle for any way that doesn't involve more trolls. Let's just run until we find a ladder or some other way up," Emily said.

"And what if we run into more trolls?"

"Let's hope that we can run faster than they can."

With a determined nod of her head, Sarah took another look down the corridors, held up a hand, and counted off on her fingers: one, two, three. As soon as her third finger was raised, she jerked Emily by the hand and they sprinted out of the door and to the left.

The girls ran until they both were panting. They chose their turns at random and stopped at each corner to make sure nothing or no one was around the other side of it before venturing onward. Emily judged by the emptiness of the tunnels and the quiet behind the closed doors that they passed that most of the trolls they had seen days before were either sleeping now or were occupied elsewhere.

Sarah looked around another corner and then led Emily into a long, lantern-lit corridor with stairs and a huge metal door at one end. The hairs on her arms stood on end and an uneasy feeling crept up her neck and onto her scalp. There was something too familiar to Emily about this tunnel, and it wasn't familiar in a good way.

Her dream.

This was the corridor that led out into the power plant on the canal, the one that was the source of all the strife between the trolls and the city government now. She could see it more clearly as the images from the dream flashed into her mind. "Wait," she said to Sarah, pulling her to a stop. "I know where we are, and I don't think it's safe for us to go that way."

"What? How do you know?"

"I dreamed about this just the other night. It was more of a nightmare, really. Those steps. I remember it now."

"Emily, it was just a dream. Those steps mean 'up', and up means *out*. Let's go!"

"But Lolfus told me that I should listen to these things," Emily said.

"I don't care what he said—I want to go home." Sarah tugged Emily, and she started moving again with much reluctance. When they reached the door, she heard the mumbled sound of voices and growls on the other side.

"No, listen!" Emily said, pointing towards the noise. They leaned in and pressed their ears against the door and looked at one another in the dim light of the lanterns. Emily could make out the sound of heavy rain falling and she looked down at her feet and saw that the stone stairs were slick with water. The feeling of déjà vu had her mind spinning.

"Hey, it's not latched," Sarah said as she slowly pushed the door open a few inches.

"This ends *now!*" they heard Malrich shout. Both girls reflexively backed away from the door at the sound of his voice. "If Tucker won't respond to the holes, Benjamin, then he'll respond to your tale of watching two young topsiders killed right before your eyes."

"That will never happen and we both know it," came a slimy response. It had to be Mr. Benjamin. "You have too much to lose."

"Do I?" Malrich taunted. "Alochar, get the prisoners!" Sarah's face grew pale as Emily tried to direct her back down the stairs with a tug of her hand.

"Quick! We need to hide!" she whispered.

Their backs were to the door when they heard, "What have we *here*?" It was Alochar, and he sounded like he would not soon forget the trick that Sarah and Emily had pulled on him earlier that night with the sleeping draught.

Alochar wasn't alone. Someone grabbed them from behind while another pair of hands tugged cloth sacks over their heads so they could see nothing, not even the glimmer of a lantern through the weave of the fabric, and bound their hands with a scratchy rope. They were hoisted off of their feet and carried in bear hugs so constricting that Emily thought she might pass out from the lack of air in her lungs. When she was released, she dropped to the muddy ground on her knees with a graceless thud.

"My, that was fast," Emily heard Malrich growl.

"They were trying to escape, my lord. Found them just inside the corridor."

"No matter. Now they're right where I want them," Malrich said. "Heinrich, come forward. You have the honor as my most valuable General of dropping the blade on these two and ending this once and for all."

Heinrich. Emily's mind immediately grasped for hope that he was as good and trustworthy as Lolfus had said, but she remembered that he made it to the position he was in because he followed orders. The sound of a long metal blade being pulled from a sheath cut through the mix of emotions that were swirling through her. She was about to cry out in protest when she heard Lolfus shout across the darkness. "No! Heinrich, ya' know this is not the answer! Bloodshed will only serve to start another war, one that will come at the cost of many lives from both sides. You're on the side of right and justice, and that's not the side Malrich stands for—his only interests are greed and power. The only thing ready to come to an end now is Malrich's reign!"

"I know what I must do," Heinrich said.

Emily felt Sarah at her side and the two huddled closer in the increasing rain and braced for the inevitable. Both were trembling and Emily thought she heard Sarah whispering a prayer or making a wish, and for some reason that simple act made the seriousness of their situation hit Emily in the gut more than any of the other events they'd gone through together in the days leading up to that moment.

She was trying to find something to say, some way to plead for their lives, to tell her friend how much she meant to her, but before any words could escape Emily's mouth, she was startled by the sounds of a struggle. There was a frenzy of shouting from the trolls combined with the *clank* of metal striking metal. Only moments after the noise had begun, the soaked cloth bag was suddenly pulled from her head and she blinked to see Heinrich and another pale troll guard engaged in a fierce swordfight with Alochar and three other trolls she didn't recognize. Malrich stood by Mr.

Benjamin and a look of fury formed on his face that made Emily's blood run cold.

"Ya' need to run—go far and fast! I'll take care of Malrich," Lolfus said, his voice right behind her. He had been the one to uncover their faces, and he worked at the rope on her wrists until finally her hands were free. She scrambled to her feet as he hurried to release Sarah's bonds.

Emily saw Heinrich run his heavy sword through the side of an opponent, causing that troll to go limp and fall at Malrich's feet. A strangled squeak of fear escaped her throat as Sarah grabbed at her hand. "Let's go!" she said.

"We *need* to help them," Emily cried. Before she could try to convince Sarah that they owed Lolfus for helping to keep them safe and then aiding in their escape, she saw him reach into his overcoat and pull out a short sword of his own. As soon as Lolfus had his weapon drawn, Malrich drew his own. The energy between the two of them felt much thicker and more malicious than the fight that was already in progress. The brothers locked eyes and shortened the distance between each other, and Emily noticed that Lolfus was careful to put himself between them and Malrich.

With a smile full of jagged teeth and his eyes gleaming wildly in the rain and faint light of the rising sun, Malrich laughed, "Thank you, brother! Now I have a reason to end your meddling, too."

CHAPTER 19

Emily and Sarah watched in horror as Lolfus, with his arm still bleeding from the blow he had received earlier, charged towards Malrich with his sword raised over his shoulder and poised to make a fierce downward strike. When the blade dropped, Malrich was swift to block it with his own, a move that sent sparks into the damp morning as the metal collided.

The brothers alternated striking and blocking as they moved farther from the girls in attempts to gain a better position. Emily had a suspicion that Lolfus was putting distance between them on purpose in another attempt to shield them from harm.

Malrich made several fast swipes toward Lolfus, missing him with each, but forcing him backward toward a fragile-looking set of iron stairs that led to an even more decrepit catwalk up above. With nowhere else to go, Lolfus had no other option apart from moving slowly up one step at a time and trying to gain the advantage over his brother's longer sword with a higher vantage point. The battle intensified, and within a few short moments the two trolls had reached the narrow walkway suspended overhead.

Emily saw Malrich make a vicious stab towards Lolfus, striking him near the shoulder of the arm that held his sword. "No!" she screamed as she sprinted toward the stairs. She climbed two steps at a time, using her arms and the rusted handrail to propel her even faster, but heard the distinct clatter of a sword on the catwalk.

Just as she reached the top of the stairs, she heard Malrich growl, "Now you die—just like Father." He raised his sword to deliver the fatal blow to his brother who lay on his back at Malrich's feet.

Emily knew that she was much higher up than she had been at Vivi's house a few days ago, and even higher than the cage she had been suspended in just hours before, but she shut all of that knowledge out as she ran for Malrich and jumped onto his back. Her arms latched around his neck with more force than she ever thought she contained. He swung madly with his free hand, but Emily was able to duck and avoid his reach. He grabbed at her wrist and tried to pry her arms from his neck, but stopped with a sudden wretch.

Her grip faltered and she fell back onto her bottom onto the crumbling catwalk. From there she saw Lolfus on his knees, still clutching the handle of his sword that he had driven through Malrich's stomach. She scrambled backward and clear of the massive troll just before he fell.

Lolfus lowered his head and took a deep breath with a pained look growing on his face, but Emily was unsure if it was because of the injuries he'd received in the battle or because of what he had just been forced to do. Before she could ask if he was okay, he reached across his brother and lifted Malrich's enormous sword above his head. He struggled to his feet and shouted to the trolls on the ground below them, "Halt! It is *done*. I hereby claim my father's sword and my rightful place as your king." The other trolls were clearly stunned, but showed their allegiance by dropping their weapons and kneeling before Lolfus regardless.

"King?" Emily whispered.

CHAPTER 20

After Lolfus helped Emily down the rickety metal stairs, she spotted Sarah leaning over Mr. Benjamin, who had curled into sort of a trembling ball, and trying to console him. "Hey, you guys! Come here! He's been mumbling something about Tucker ever since the fighting started," Sarah called to them.

Benjamin whimpered and squeaked when he saw Lolfus approach him. "Mr. Benjamin, I mean ya' no harm. Whatever your part in all of this, I just intend to put a stop to the fighting and restore the terms of the agreement between my people and yours. Now, what's this ya' were saying about the mayor?"

Skepticism played across the man's face and threatened to settle there. Apparently his prior dealings with Malrich had given him good reason to be suspicious and untrusting of anything a troll said to him, but he must have seen the sincerity that Lolfus possessed because he eventually relaxed a little. After a deep breath and a pleading look toward Sarah and then to Emily, he managed to speak. "I...I've helped Tucker with the development plans for the power plant since the beginning. He won't pull back because he stands to make over a million dollars from the developer when the project is complete."

"You mean the *city* will make a million when it's all done, right?" Sarah asked.

Lolfus continued to watch the man very carefully, and then he said, "No, I think he means that Tucker himself will be cashing in on the deal. Am I right, Mr. Benjamin?"

Benjamin nodded like a huge weight had just been lifted from his shoulders and then began to sob hysterically. Between blubbering wails, he said, "I...I arranged the deal. He was getting a kickback from the developer to make sure that the zoning and all of the other permits were passed without any trouble. I was going to get a bonus for setting it up." After he got all of the words out, the sobbing continued. Emily suspected the slimy, tough-guy persona that she'd seen from him on television so many times before was just an act. She wasn't sure if she should feel sorry for him or if she should find amusement in how much his current state contrasted with the one he presented to the public.

"It's okay," Lolfus said. "I think if ya' have something in writing between the mayor and that developer to prove what ya' just told me, we can put this thing to rest and put Tucker where he belongs—in jail."

"In m-m-my briefcase," Mr. Benjamin sputtered. He stretched out an arm and pointed with a shaking hand at a brown leather case lying in the mud just a few yards away from him. The rain had slowed to barely a drizzle, but Emily expected that any papers in that briefcase were probably soaked by now. She popped open the shiny brass latches and found that everything inside was still dry and undamaged. After flipping through a few pages, she found a signed agreement that would seal Tucker's fate without a doubt. He had abused his position as mayor, entered into illegal contracts with shady developers, and put countless lives in danger by ignoring the treaty with the trolls all because of his own greed.

Emily swallowed her disgust with Tucker for the moment and looked to Lolfus. "He's right—it's here," she said.

"Well, then. I have no quarrel with Mr. Benjamin here. As soon as that proof is handed over to the authorities and the charges are filed against Tucker, I suppose he'll have to answer to the topsiders and accept whatever punishment they decide to hand down. Isn't that right, Mr. Benjamin?" Lolfus said.

Benjamin only wailed louder and covered his face with his arms like a child having a tantrum. "I'll take that as a yes," Sarah said as she rolled her eyes.

Lolfus ordered the troll guards to leave Mr. Benjamin there to work out whatever he needed to and then let him find his own way back to his office. Heinrich volunteered to coordinate moving Malrich to the Great Hall and seeing to the start of his funeral arrangements. Emily could see that it was an enormous relief to Lolfus that his friend was willing to do this. It seemed that even though Malrich had killed their father to assume his power and was willing to do the same to Lolfus, he was still grieving the loss of his brother. The loss of his brother at his own hand made that death even more difficult to bear.

Emily carried Mr. Benjamin's briefcase and she and Sarah followed Lolfus and two of the troll guards back into the tunnels. They walked for what felt like forever until they came upon the hum of activity in the marketplace. One of the guards broke away from the group and quickly moved to the other guards who had been standing watch over the market to tell them about the events that had just transpired outside.

Lolfus stopped in the center of the cavernous room, Malrich's sword in his hand, and waited for the echoing trumpet of a horn that silenced the vast space. His voice boomed above the crowd, "Malrich is no longer your leader—his reign has come to an end. I, Lolfus, eldest son of Baldemar the Red, take my rightful place as your king." For a moment, all went silent, and then the room suddenly erupted with cheers and celebration.

Lolfus turned to Sarah and Emily amidst the noise and strained to shout, "I suppose ya' would like to be getting home now?" They were so relieved and excited at the prospect that all they could do was smile in response.

CHAPTER 21

Lolfus carried a lantern and led Emily and Sarah through the long and maze-like tunnels with a guard following closely behind them. Emily thought it would probably take Lolfus a while to get used to the idea of having someone follow him everywhere for his own safety. It seemed strange that someone so large would need a bodyguard, especially when that bodyguard was nearly a foot shorter than the troll he was supposed to be protecting. She chuckled at the thought and then listened in on the conversation already in progress between Lolfus and Sarah.

"So, you think things will be okay now? No more holes?" Sarah asked.

"I *know* things will be okay. The gnomes answer to me now, and I'm not giving any orders for more chaos. Besides, after ya' drop off those papers, Tucker will be out of office and this whole matter will just be another scandal for the city records."

They walked uphill and into a room of intersecting tunnels that looked slightly familiar. It was the roundhouse where they had first bumped into Lolfus after falling into the sinkhole. It felt to Emily like time had done something weird since they went underground, like it had stretched out into one long night instead of the passing of several. She was sure there was no way a person could get used to never seeing the sunlight.

"Do ya' understand the plan?" he asked the girls. Both nodded in unison. "Alright then." Lolfus raised a hand and pounded out a strange rhythm on one of the doors in the roundhouse. They all exchanged looks in silence as they waited for a response. Just as Lolfus lifted an arm to prepare to knock again, they heard the sliding and clicking of several locks and latches on the opposite side.

The door swung in just a few inches and the beam of a flashlight shone out, "Can I help you?" a deep voice said.

Lolfus cleared his throat, "Yes, I hope so. These two seem to have gotten themselves lost, said they fell in a sinkhole. Can you take them through?"

The door opened wider and the flashlight's beam fell to Emily and Sarah, forcing them to squint and squirm. "Oh, my... Oh..." the voice said. As her eyes began to adjust, Emily could make out an older man's face, and moments later she saw that the man was wearing some sort of uniform. "Of course, of course!"

"Girls, this is the door that leads into the old church. We've had friends here for a very long time, and I trust that you're in good hands. Isn't that right, sir?" Lolfus said.

"Yes, certainly," the man said. "I'm David Green. Are you girls okay? The whole city has been looking for you."

"Just tired, hungry, and ready to go home," Emily said. They watched as Mr. Green fumbled with the radio clipped at his shoulder with shaking hands to call for police and paramedics to Monumental Church. He tried to explain that he found the two missing girls, but the radio commotion of codes and call signs that began after that made it too difficult to understand what exactly was happening.

Emily turned to Lolfus. "Thank you, and I really am sorry about your brother. I wish it could have ended differently."

"So do I. Still, I couldn't have stopped that madness without the help from ya' both, and things are far better now because of it. Better than ya' truly know. Go on now, but remember if ya' ever need anything, just tell a stone wall or a stone road and the message will get to me fast as light. I'm in your debt." Lolfus said.

"Tell a *what*?" Sarah asked.

Lolfus couldn't hold back a laugh, and the lantern he held bounced and clanked with each of his breaths. "The gnomes—they'll hear ya' and they'll tell me right away. You're in the network now," he said with a wink.

Mr. Green looked slightly horrified and thoroughly confused as both of the girls sandwiched Lolfus in a hug so tight that he was nearly struggling for air. When they finally released him and stepped through the door into an musty-smelling basement, they looked back to see both Lolfus and his guard smiling and waving in the soft light of the railway lantern.

The moment the guard closed the door and began fastening all of the locks, they heard dozens of sirens approaching from a distance. "Hurry, we need to get you two upstairs! Did he explain things? No mention of *them*, right?" he asked.

"Right," Sarah and Emily said in chorus.

"Okay, now follow me," he said. "Oh, and you should probably figure out soon how to explain that briefcase."

CHAPTER 22

Emily was sure that her parents were going to crush her, that is, if they didn't suffocate her first.

She had been home almost twelve hours and they still wouldn't let her out of their sight. Max even looked a little happy to see her, even though she knew that he would never admit to it.

Her entire afternoon had been filled with police asking questions and emergency medical personnel checking her multiple times for injuries. Everyone was throwing around words like "miracle" and "amazing" when they talked about how she and Sarah had managed to withstand the fall down that ragged sinkhole without so much as a broken bone, but *then* to survive days in those collapsing tunnels with no food or water. Of course, she and Sarah had intentionally left out the part about the tasty homemade bread and Hostess cupcakes.

"So, tell me again, you and Sarah went back to the edge of the sinkhole and you saw a briefcase down there?" her mom said.

"Yep. It looked pretty expensive, so we thought it must be important and that maybe we should try and fish it out. And, well, you know how *that* ended. Apparently we nearly got ourselves killed *and* got the mayor fired in the same week."

"Hey, it's a good thing you had all of that stuff in your backpack to help you out down there. Like I always say—it's better to have it and not need it then to need it and not have it," her dad said.

Emily and her mother exchanged eye rolls. "The mayor's mess isn't your fault. What matters is that you and Sarah made it home safe and," her mom said. "Now, tell me all about what it was like in those tunnels!"

- The End -

CPSIA information can be obtained at www.ICGtesting.com
Printed in the USA
BVOW03s0013221013

334297BV00001B/4/P